About the author: I live in Cumbria I have been writing for many years.
My novels are a mix of romance, drama & comedy.
My interests are music, writing, reading, theatre, films & travelling around the UK.

You can find me on Twitter AlexStone@glitter452
Instagram solsburyhill355

Also available by the same author

English Girl Irish Heart
Glamour Girl
Spotlight
Love
American Dreams
Chasing Rainbows

This novel is a work of fiction the names characters & incidents portrayed are the author's imagination any resemblance to anyone living or dead is purely coincidental.

First published in Great Britain 2023

Printed & bound in Great Britain

Happy times

Polly had returned to New York for Christmas with her best friend Maggie it was nearly Christmas.
Everyone was loved up except Maggie who was single.
She still liked her ex-boyfriend Max but didn't want them to go out again Maggie wanted to find love.
Polly was planning a baby she and her partner Margie had started talking about starting a family together.
She'd been thinking about it for the first time in years she had two daughters with her ex-wife Corey.
And her son Luke he was now twenty three Polly still didn't feel old enough to have a twenty three year old son.
As she was only in her late thirties their relationship wasn't great he still resented her for not being there.
Due to her movie career that it was because of her glamour shoots hours on films sets and chat shows.
Which meant they could live in a nice house wear designer clothes and go on holiday.
She would have felt the same as he did at her age but he didn't even want to give her a chance.
To explain things their relationship was almost non-existent Luke preferred her mum Sarah.

She had brought him up in Liverpool away from Hollywood Polly didn't approve of his friends.
None of them seemed to have much enthusiasm to do anything except play computer games.
Where as she was well read loved the theatre she found it hard having a son so different from her.
Polly had been trying not to give up on their relationship.
Visiting Liverpool it was hard having a son who wasn't interested in her.
And her relationship with her mum was love hate.
Whatever happened having a baby would be a nice idea.
Margie had always wanted a daughter after having two sons Polly wanted a little boy after having two girls.
She was secure in her relationship with Margie.
And knew more about life Polly wasn't sure if she could get pregnant but was willing to give it a try.
They hadn't told anyone of their plans yet they needed to find a father one day they visited Andy.
Polly's ex-husband who she was still good friends with.
At his house in Essex as they told him their plans asking what he thought.
Polly was surprised when he suggested himself she wondered what Marcee Andy's wife would say.
If she knew Andy said she wouldn't find out.

And it meant her daughter Marie and the baby would be half-brother and sister it sounded like the perfect idea.
They didn't tell anyone of their plans but they hoped it wouldn't take too long.
Polly decided to spend Christmas in New York she'd invited Corey over they were still good friends.
And it was she who had helped get her and Margie together and who didn't love New York at Christmas.
Stacey would be staying in Liverpool with Kaleigh.
Stacey was Polly's other best friend they'd known each other since they were thirteen.
They were also family by marriage Stacey's Aunt Wendy had once been married to Polly's dad Simon.
Kaleigh's was Polly's younger sister as Corey read the e-mail on her computer it was from Polly.
Inviting her to spend Christmas in New York she wasn't sure but thought why not she was single.
And she had no-one to spend Christmas with of course Corey knew she could have gone to her mum's.
Or her brother Daniel's house but she couldn't miss the opportunity to spend Christmas in New York.
Polly had said she should invite Daniel and her son Douglas over Corey thought it was a good idea.

Of course they said yes all her family together at Christmas it would be great.
As Corey arrived in New York she was happy and couldn't wait to go ice skating at the Rockefeller Center.
And see the Christmas trees go shopping in Macy's.
See all the Christmas things she had lived in America for a few years but had moved back to Ireland.
A taxi took them from the airport to Polly's apartment.
As they watched New York lit up at night it felt magical.
Polly had made everything look nice Corey rang the doorbell Polly opened 'Cor' she hugged her.
'Glad to see you back in New York' 'me too'.
'That's why I invited you over I thought we could have a nice Christmas hi Dan' he gave Polly a hug.
'Thanks for inviting us' 'anytime' 'hi Dougie' 'hi'.
'Come in let me help you with your things' she and Polly got along even better than when they were married.
That evening they had a drink chatted it was great.
The next day Corey went out shopping with Daniel and Douglas there was only a few days left till Christmas.
Polly and Margie looked after Susan and Marie while they were out as expected it was busy.
Corey brought herself a long dark green coat with gold buttons in Macy's she looked great.

It had cost three hundred dollars Douglas and Daniel looked at the gadget department.
As Corey looked at jewellery she held up some silver hoop earrings to a mirror.
Next to her a man asked the assistant how much a watch was Corey recognised his voice it was Steve.
Her ex-boyfriend and a good friend for many years they'd met in New York while starring in a movie together.
'Steve' 'Corey how are you?' 'I'm great' 'fancy seeing you here this is great I was just thinking about you'.
'A few days ago you look great as always' 'that green coat's really nice it matches your eyes' 'thanks it's new'.
'So you're here in New York' 'I'm staying with Polly and Margie her wife I'm single'.
'I thought I've got nothing left to lose and you can't beat New York at Christmas' 'is it me or do you never age'.
'I swear you haven't changed since we first met'.
'Neither have you' Corey said 'I just had botox I went to someone good none of that frozen look' 'you look great'.
'Do you have a girlfriend?' Corey asked 'I've been on some dates no-one special I tried speed dating'.
'How did it go?' 'really bad a disaster a minute is not long enough to know someone I'm ok I'm getting too old'.

'For the dating scene' 'I feel the same' 'I have other things to keep me occupied I'm going ice skating tonight'.
'At the Rockefeller Center wanna come?' Steve asked.
'I'd love to Daniel hello again' 'hi' 'hi Dougie how old are you now?' 'Dougie's twenty two now'.
'Well you look great on it' 'thanks' 'Steve invited me ice skating to the Rockefeller Center tonight'.
'You should all come there's always a great atmosphere at Christmas' 'we'd love to' Corey replied 'that's great'.
'We'll see you then bye Steve' he kissed her on the cheek.
She was taken aback 'he still fancies you' Daniel said.
'Well it's in the past' 'must be that green coat you're wearing' 'well he said he's been speed dating recently'.
'I bet at the time you thought he was special you were probably just a notch on his bedpost'.
'He's still my friend it was a while ago can we talk about something else' 'of course'.
'We'll find you a new girlfriend in no time' Corey was angry at her brother for his comment.
She didn't believe she'd been a notch on Steve's bedpost.
He'd told her she was special he'd even asked her twice to marry him which she declined Steve told her he loved her.
When they'd gone out together she didn't know for sure.
Maybe he'd had other serious relationships like that.

She'd always counted Steve as a good friend.
That evening Corey was in good spirits she was excited about going to see Steve at the Rockefeller Center.
Dougie was too as he loved ice skating Polly and Margie had also come along it would be fun as everyone skated.
To the music 'having a good time?' Steve said to Corey.
'The best' 'I'm glad I saw you' 'me too I'll see you in a minute' she went to find Douglas.
Who had a problem with his skates Daniel decided to speak to Steve alone 'hey I'm glad you could come'.
'So are we' 'maybe it's not my place to say this I care a lot about my sister' 'I know that'.
'I don't want her being a notch on your bedpost'.
'I don't know what you mean' 'I know you still fancy her'.
'I want her to be with someone really nice' 'I care about Corey as a good friend' 'whatever your feelings for her'.
'She's a lesbian she can't change her sexuality'.
'I know that she's just a friend' 'good she needs good friends' Corey returned to the rink.
She couldn't see Steve Corey wondered where he was.
'Steve's gone' Corey said 'well don't worry'.
'I'm here to keep you company' Daniel smiled.

Corey waited ten minutes she tried to hide her disappointment that Steve had left.
Later after they'd finished their ice skating session she saw him chatting to a woman with blonde hair.
He'd obviously been on a date at the same time.
She should have realised she'd had a good time
Corey went back to Polly's had an early night.
She was going to text Steve but she changed her mind.
He would have been too busy to worry about her the next morning Corey felt good.
Christmas was only a few days away Polly made her lunch
'Cor why did you never tell me about you and Steve'.
'I assumed it was a one night stand Daniel told me'.
'It was a relationship after we split up' 'it was a fling'.
'That's all I felt down about us splitting up' 'I suppose we've all done things we regret'.
'In case you're wondering I'm not bi it was a one off'.
'I understand' Corey felt ashamed for referring to her relationship with Steve as a fling she had loved him.
The only relationship she ever regretted was Amy.
Her ex-girlfriend when she was a teenager. Corey couldn't have her brother finding out how she really felt.
She felt angry at him as to why he'd told Polly about such an old relationship from five years before.

She suspected he was slightly jealous there had never been a man in her life he wanted that role as her brother.
And best friend maybe he saw Steve as a threat he had no reason to as December 23rd came around Corey felt ill.
And felt light headed and hot she was sure she was coming down with a virus.
Corey decided to go to a cocktail bar in Manhattan with Margie and Polly she took some paracetamol.
Wearing more make-up than usual wearing a black glittery dress 1920's style and a black bag to match.
She looked good even if she felt ill Maggie was in good spirits Margie had fallen ill so wasn't with them.
Corey felt ok as they ventured into the bar it had green lamps with a gold trim which lit up the room.
With brown marble pillars it reminded Corey of London she just wanted a quiet night she ordered an orange juice.
As she sat at the bar 'nice isn't it?' Polly said 'it's great'.
'I'll be with Maggie back soon' Corey watched everyone talking 'hey' 'Steve' 'fancy seeing you here again'.
'I'm here with Polly and Maggie' 'not your brother' 'no'.
'He's pretty protective of you' 'what do you mean?'.
'He said some things the other night at the ice rink'.
'What things?' 'that he didn't want you to be a notch on my bedpost' 'I can't believe he said that'.

'He also said you deserve to be with someone who treats you right it's no secret I don't think much of your brother'.
'I promise I won't come on to you' 'you're a really good friend to me' 'don't worry about Daniel'.
'He's protective of me because of how it was when we were growing up he's always been the only man in my life'.
'Except Louie who's gay he sees you as a threat please ignore whatever he said' 'let's have a drink to friendship'.
Steve said 'to friendship' 'I like the dress' 'I like you're top how did your date go? the other night' 'what date?'.
'I saw you with a blonde woman at the ice rink'.
'Oh no that was my sister I'm enjoying not being in a relationship' 'me too' 'hey' Polly said joining them.
'Hi Steve' 'hi I happened to bump into Corey'
'do you come here often?' Polly asked 'sometimes'.
'It's a nice quiet place to relax I'm thinking of moving here permanently I'm sick of L.A' 'oh right'.
'Too much temptation for an ex-alcoholic like me'.
'I've always loved New York' 'what's with the mistletoe?' Corey asked 'you and Steve should have a kiss' 'what?'.
'Why not?' Polly held up the mistletoe as they kissed.
'What about you you've not kissed anyone you could kiss Steve' Maggie suggested to Polly.
'It's been so long since I kissed a man'.

'Then let Steve refresh your memory' Maggie said Polly kissed Steve it was fun 'you'll be reverting soon'.
Maggie joked 'no I know my sexuality women only'.
'I bet there's loads of your male fans out there that would love to get you into bed' Maggie said 'let them fantasize'.
They laughed 'Mags I think you're drunk' 'maybe'.
Corey had enjoyed her night out despite not feeling herself.
She was annoyed that her brother had said things to Steve clearly jealous of their friendship the next day she felt ill.
And she couldn't even go to midnight mass as she usually did Christmas was ruined.
Polly and Daniel looked after her making her vegetable soup and honey and lemon tea.
Besides there was always next year a few days later Corey felt better she flew home to Dublin.
She couldn't go out New Years Eve as she wasn't up to it.
She would have loved to have seen the fireworks in London with Stacey.
Corey watched Jools Holland Hootenanny on BBC2.
There was always next year and she couldn't stop thinking about her kiss with Steve even if he was single.
He just wanted to be friends Corey knew she shouldn't have been thinking about him.

She thought her feelings for him were gone she should have been looking for a woman.
And Corey knew she'd never have again what she'd had with Polly she'd been in love with Stacey.
Corey knew she'd missed her chance Kaleigh was her wife she couldn't face another marriage gone wrong.
Maybe she should stop looking for love lots of women stayed single for years maybe life would be easier.
Less complicated she thought.
On February 14th her bandmate Kitty and brother Daniel were due to get married in Edinburgh they loved the city.
They were getting married in the castle.
In one of the special wedding rooms all the band would be there as well as Colin Douglas's father.
And an old friend of her's and her mother Carol and step-dad John as well as Stacey, Polly, Margie and Louie.
As they finally arrived in Edinburgh they arrived at their lovely five star hotel Kitty had her wedding dress.
Daniel his suit Corey couldn't wait to see her brother get married Daniel and Kitty made a great couple.
Hopefully they'd find happiness together Corey was happy with her hotel room Polly had checked in with Margie.
Colin was also due to arrive as well as Carol and John.

They all loved Edinburgh and were looking forward to the wedding Corey had invited Steve along.
With his best friend Kieran they were always saying how much they wanted to visit Scotland.
As Kieran was half-Scottish Corey also hoped Daniel would apologise for what he'd said about Steve.
She freshened up reapplying her foundation and eyeshadow she felt better as she sprayed some perfume.
She wore a Quiz emerald green glittery dress and some stud earrings as Corey went to the bar area.
As she ordered herself a lemonade she chatted to Kitty.
Who was also there 'excited for tomorrow' Corey asked.
'Yeah I am it'll be a great day I only wished dad could have been here' 'I'm sure he's looking down'.
Corey looked over as Daniel and Mike came towards them 'what the hell is going on!' Daniel said angry.
Looking at Corey 'why is Steve and his friend here?'.
'I invited them' 'why?' 'Steve's a good friend' 'come on'.
'That ship sailed a long time ago I'm only interested in women in fact I'm not interested in anyone'.
'You shouldn't have invited him or his friend!' 'Kieran said he always wanted to visit Scotland' 'or Ireland'.
'Or anywhere else you happen to be!' 'he's with Kieran'.
'It's my wedding you know that!'.

'So I don't get to choose who I get invite to my own wedding now!' 'Steve's just a friend nothing else'.
'Who wants to get into bed with you!' 'Dan!' Kitty said. Trying to calm him down 'I have no interest in having sex with Steve or any other man I promise'.
'We had a one off relationship that was it why can't you let me move on!' 'you should apologise for what you said'.
'No Kitty it's the truth!' 'please stop being jealous!'.
Corey said 'I don't think so unlike some men I treat women with respect! you don't need people like him around!'.
'He's a friend nothing else!' 'you're my sister I'm looking out for you' 'hey everyone we've just arrived' 'Louie!'.
Corey was glad he'd come so he could lighten the mood.
'Come in let's chill out' Kitty said as they chatted as Corey was forced to pretend she felt ok.
Instead she was angry at her brother later that evening she paid Steve a visit as she knocked on his door.
'Come in' 'hi I saw you earlier at the bar I didn't want to get into anything with your brother' 'you're my friend'.
'Louie's here now it should be ok I can hang out with whoever I want forget what he said please come over'.
Kitty's one of my best friends' 'we will then' 'so how are you liking Edinburgh?' 'great hotel great city'.
'Maybe tomorrow you can see it better in daylight'

'I hope so I love Europe' Kieran said 'anytime you want me to go just say you must be tired'.
'After your long journey' 'you can stay as long as you want' 'Steve's right listen I'm going back to the bar'.
'Coming?' Kieran asked 'give me one minute' Steve said.
'Ok see you there' Kieran left 'I missed you' 'I'm sorry about what Daniel said in New York' 'really it's ok'.
'Daniel not here I love my brother he looks out for me but it's my life I can see talk to who I want to'.
'Can I give you a hug?' Steve asked 'of course' they looked at each other 'you're so pretty' 'no' 'yes'.
Corey leaned over to kiss Steve she didn't care anymore.
She wasn't going to fight her desires lesbian or not he kissed her back passionately 'we can't be too long'.
'Everyone's downstairs at the bar' Corey said 'you're right' Corey and Steve arrived at the bar.
Pretending as if nothing had happened inside she felt great amazing on cloud nine buzzing.
Was it wrong that she was attracted to Steve they were both single they chatted with everyone at the bar.
Everyone was happy and excited about the wedding the next day that evening Corey lay in bed.
As she stared at the ceiling thinking about her kiss with Steve how she wished she could do it all again.

If only she had her own hotel room she was sharing with Kitty as it was bad luck for the groom to see the bride.
The next morning Corey woke early so she could have her hair and make-up done for the wedding.
Corey was wearing a mint green dress her other friend Mary was a bridesmaid and Kitty's sister.
Kitty looked beautiful they were getting married in the Queen Anne room which had a red carpet with red seats.
With crème bows tied at the back as Kitty entered she looked lovely with her ivory beaded wedding dress.
Daniel wore a black suit and white shirt the bridesmaids looked beautiful wearing mint green dresses.
After they had their wedding reception in the Jacobite room it had red walls and a wooden ceiling.
With a cosy feeling Daniel made a speech as he talked of Corey as his best friend.
The only woman he had ever loved besides his wife.
She was still angry as she thought he had overreacted to Steve he'd only apologised because he had to.
Because Kitty had made him but at least there would be no fighting they posed for photos outside Edinburgh Castle.
The weather had been nice it had been a good day and it was always good to catch up with her mum.
And Colin that evening there was a disco inside the hotel.

She and Colin danced together it reminded her of being thirteen when they'd first met Steve joined them.
'This is Colin this is Steve my good friend from America'.
'How are you?' 'Colin's Dougie's father' 'he seems like a lovely young man' 'he is I'm proud of him'.
'Congratulations on the Grand National'.
'It was a few years ago thanks' Corey was happy.
Why couldn't Daniel get on with Steve like Colin did she was having a great night being with people she loved.
Later she went to see Steve Corey had a kiss with Steve.
The next day after the wedding Steve and Kieran flew back to the states Corey went home to Dublin.
She'd had a nice time with Steve maybe it would be better to leave it the way her love life had gone.
Since splitting with Polly.
Polly was excited about planning a baby with Margie she'd done two tests so far nothing had happened.
She wondered if it was an age thing Andy was in his early fifties she was now thirty five while still young.
She wasn't twenty one anymore either Polly thought a baby would be nice.
If it didn't happen it wouldn't be the end of the world.
Polly had another thing to keep her busy since she'd found out Kaleigh had a daughter.

Who she'd had as a teenager she'd wanted to find her.
Polly looked online for information but there were lots of Amy's from Liverpool.
She decided to call her old social worker Carla for a chat.
To see if she could help her with her enquires.

Polly & Vanya

Polly knew her files were confidential but surely she could make an exception.
As they chatted one day Carla said she wasn't sure.
'Polly please I shouldn't really be doing this giving you this information' 'please listen no-one will ever find out'.
'What if they do what if I lose my job?' 'they won't no-one will ever know I promise I won't tell anyone'.
'It's not like I'm gonna go over to her house say who I am'.
'I just want to know she's ok maybe a photo see what she looks like she is my niece' 'alright yes ok' 'thanks'.
'I know I'm asking a lot of you working for social services I'm grateful for your help' 'ok Polly chat soon' 'thanks'.
Polly put the phone down happy at her good news.
'What's going on?' it was her mum 'nothing' 'your niece'.
'I'm guessing you weren't referring to Christian and Stacey's kids I know Kaleigh had a baby I used to visit'.
'Before she was taken away it was Shaun's idea'.
'Sue wanted to keep the baby he had a temper so it was for the best I've only just found out myself'.
'Did she told you anything?' 'my social worker she's given me an address I don't know what to do'.
'The father who was he? some lad' 'yeah'.

'Her first boyfriend' Polly lied she felt awful having to lie.
About the fact Shaun Kaleigh's step-uncle and the man who had helped raise her along with their Aunt Sue.
Had raped Kaleigh as a teeanger if her mum knew the truth it would upset her 'so she had the baby adopted?'.
'Yeah she called her Amy she was thirteen'.
Her mum explained 'if she's given you this address you should check it out' 'yeah why not' Polly replied.
'I just can't believe you never said that she had a baby'.
'You were away working doing glamour modelling'.
'And your movie career' 'Kaleigh she was too young to have a baby' 'I know you're right'.
A few days later Polly decided to check out the address herself a taxi dropped her off it was a nice area.
Which made her feel better the house had double glazing.
A white door gold knocker nice flower Polly looked around hoping no-one would think she was a burglar.
Come to check out the house she walked near the door glancing through the window curiously.
An elderly woman with short grey hair approached her.
'Are you looking for Vanya?' 'yeah' 'she's at the park'.
'Where is it?' 'not far just round the corner' 'thanks'.
'Anytime' Polly was happy she had a lead in her search for her niece Vanya must have been her adoptive mum.
She headed round the corner it was a nice medium sized park Polly stood nearby watching.
Keeping a distance she watched mums with kids.

As she wondered which one was her niece Polly
saw a red head curly haired girl.
Which she assumed she was Kaleigh's daughter.
She ventured inside the park sitting down her eye was
drawn to a slightly overweight girl.
With medium brown curly hair and pale skin.
Her mum had blonde straight hair blue eyes and wore
a black mac she looked at Polly for a moment.
'Hi you're not…you can't be Polly Patterson'.
'Yeah it's me' 'oh my god! I'm such a big fan' 'thanks'.
'So you're here in Liverpool' 'I have a house in
the Wirral' 'it's a good area' 'yeah'.
'I was checking out good parks for my daughter Susan'.
'It's good here all the mum's are really nice it's quite safe'.
'That's good' Vanya was joined by the girl with curly
brown hair 'she's yours' 'yes this is Harmony she's ten'.
'She's gorgeous does the dad have curly hair?'.
'I don't know she's adopted I couldn't have kids I tried
IVF in the end I decided to adopt'.
'They said her mum was a teenager just a kid too young
to look after her'.
'They said they didn't know who the dad was'.
'Do you have a husband?' Polly asked 'I did once we split
when she was three we don't talk much it's a shame'.
'But she's got my brother her uncle we're really close'.
'That's nice she's got family around' 'yeah I love her
so much she's such a well behaved little girl'.

'Really shy but bright she's got mild dyslexia but it was picked up early'.
'I'm hoping if she works hard she can overcome it'.
'There's all these adult education classes nowadays'.
'It's amazing meeting you you're really pretty'.
'Thanks I've got to go but it's been good meeting you'.
'I'm here Fridays afternoons' 'I might see you again bye'.
'Bye Polly' she would have loved to have stayed longer to chat but Polly hoped she could visit the park again.
She was so happy to have seen her niece she was gorgeous and seemed sweet.
Luckily she looked more like Kaleigh than Shaun.
Her pretty face pale skin but her dark curly hair from Shaun who was mixed-race.
Maybe it was better she had been adopted under the circumstances.
Polly was sure her mum would want to see her.
The following Friday she arranged for her mum to see Harmony at the park.
At the same time as the week before she was sure her mum would be happy to see her.
'Are you sure this is a good idea?' Sarah asked 'yeah'.
'Of course' 'I feel like that storyline in Emmerdale stalking the adoptive mother if she finds out we're here' 'it's fine'.
'Vanya doesn't know we have anything to do with her'.
'What if she gets suspicious' 'she won't if you act normal'.
'This is stalking' 'no it's not'.

'Two grown women hanging around in a park for no good reason' 'mum this is your grandchild we're talking about'.
'Alright then just to have a look' 'well I can't wait to see Harmony again' Polly said smiling.
She knew once her mum saw Harmony she'd love her.
'Are you sure this isn't a wasted journey' 'it's her'.
Polly looked over at Vanya she appeared with Harmony.
'Which one?' 'the woman with blonde hair' 'Polly'.
'This is my mum Sarah' 'hello there' 'I wanted to show mum the park' 'I'm so happy to see you again Polly'.
'Me too' 'well it's not every day I meet a celebrity'.
'I don't think of myself like that I prefer meeting the general public you've brought Harmony again' 'yeah'.
'I'm looking after my friends little boy this afternoon'.
'She can push him on the swings' Polly saw her mum's face light up as she looked at Harmony 'she's lovely'.
'Thanks' 'love that coat' Polly worried her mum was being too obvious that Vanya would guess who they were.
'My daughter Susan's seven not far off her age'.
'Oh I'm dreading big school in a year once they get there their not kids anymore mobiles phones all that'.
'To look forward' 'is her dad around?' 'mum!'.
'I didn't mean it like that I meant today' 'it's fine no she doesn't see much of her dad'.
'Well I bet you do an amazing job' Polly said trying to change the subject 'thanks Polly' they chatted for a bit.

After half an hour Polly knew they should go even if she really wanted to stay 'it's been so nice chatting' 'you too'. Polly said 'anytime you wanna come round for a cup of tea here's my mobile' 'I'd love to thanks' Polly was happy. Now she could get to know Harmony better as they went home.
Polly knew she and her mum would have things to talk about 'well what did you think?' 'Vanya's really nice'.
'No Harmony' 'she's gorgeous I can't believe she's my grand daughter' 'I knew you'd love her'.
'I wish we could say who we are' 'we can't' 'why not?'.
'Because you've only met her twice it's too soon'.
'Mum' 'I'm happy we've seen her' 'I knew you'd love her'.
'And Vanya' 'I do but…' 'but what?' 'if Vanya knew you were Harmony's Aunt' 'she doesn't'.
'What do you think she would say?' 'I'm sure she wouldn't mind' 'you know that's not true I know if that was me'.
'I'd be pissed off' 'why?' 'Susie you adopt a child you want that child all to yourself'.
'Without any family members around' 'mum!' 'no hear me out just before your child'.
'Is about to start secondary school the child's Aunt and grandmother turn up it might not seem like a big deal'.
'But how do you think Vanya would feel'
'she wouldn't mind' 'she'd be worried'.
'In case we're trying to take Harmony away from her'.
'We're not I just wanted to see what she looked like'.

'That she's ok' 'now you have you should leave her alone'.
'Has Kaleigh asked you to track her down?' 'no'.
'Well then' 'she's my niece' 'Kaleigh is still only twenty one she's not old enough to deal with this'.
'Don't tell me you didn't feel love for her like I did'.
'Of course I did more than anything which is why this stops now before we get anymore involved'.
'Before she finds out who we are' 'she won't' 'Polly'.
'How would you feel if you adopted a child and a few years later her family appeared wanting access to her'.
'You'd feel jealous threatened' 'I've seen her now' 'yes and you know she's well cared for by a nice woman'.
'So let's end it now when she's eighteen and decides to track down Kaleigh she'll know we're here for her'.
'Nothing until then ok I know it's hard but you know it's the right thing to do you can't come back to this park again'.
'Alright' 'you don't contact Vanya again however tempting it is Harmony was adopted and she's having a nice life'.
'We can rest easy' 'ok fine I'll leave it' deep down Polly knew she was right but it still upset her.
That she wouldn't be able to see Harmony again that night she thought about things she was upset.
At never seeing Harmony again but knew she had no choice the next day she decided to go shopping.
Take her mind off things it didn't work Polly thought of Vanya and Harmony she didn't stay long.
As Polly walked outside she saw Vanya 'Polly' 'hi'.

'Fancy seeing you again' Vanya said happy to see her.
'I know' 'fancy coming for a milkshake?' 'I can't'.
'Why not?' 'I'm so sorry' Polly cried as she walked away.
'What's wrong? you seem upset' 'I'm a bad person'.
'Sit down tell me' 'you'll hate me when I tell you'.
'A problem shared is a problem halved' 'I'm not who you think I am' 'what do you mean?' 'I lied to you'.
'I didn't meet you in a park by accident'.
'What do you mean?' 'an old woman told me where you were I wasn't stalking I just wanted to see her one time'.
'I don't understand' 'Harmony's my niece'.
'Kaleigh's you know her birth mum I'm sorry if I've upset you I promise you won't have to see me again'.
'Please don't cry' 'I didn't mean to lie about it'.
'I just wanted to see what she looked like if she looked liked Kaleigh or her dad' 'you don't have to be upset'.
'I would have done the same thing I'm happy you told me I know who her birth mum is now'.
'You're a good mum' 'I try to be so Kaleigh was thirteen'.
'Yeah she wouldn't have coped she has mild learning difficulties ADHD dyslexia a stammer epilepsy'.
'You wouldn't know it looking at her she's the sweetest person my sister' 'does she know? you met Harmony' 'no'.
'We only discussed it once she said she didn't think her daughter would want to know her'.
'Why she'd been adopted' 'well don't worry'.
'I'll make sure she knows Kaleigh loved her'.

'She really did she was a few weeks old when she was adopted it was for the best'.
'Everything happens for a reason you don't have to worry you won't hear from us again mum said it was bad'.
'What we did that you'd feel upset threatened' 'no Polly'.
'I would have done the same and I really like you and you can see Harmony any time you like' 'are you sure?' 'yes'.
'Thanks' 'if you're not busy you can come round I have my brother but he's often busy working away'.
'So it would be nice for Harmony to see her Aunt I'm not angry I'm happy I met you' 'thanks I'm glad I met you' Polly knew her mum wouldn't approve but she didn't care.
Only a few days later she went round to see Vanya again at 6pm 'hi come in this is my house' 'it's very nice'.
'I'm glad you like it drink?' 'yes please' 'orange juice'.
'That'll be great' Polly made herself feel at home there were lots of photos of Harmony red candles and a Buddha.
Corey would have loved it with her spiritual interests.
'This is so weird me having tea with a celebrity'.
'I don't think of myself like that I have one or two celeb friends but that's it' 'well you can come round anytime'.
'Harmony will be back soon she's at dance class'.
'What dancing?' 'tap she hated ballet' 'Kaleigh was dancing from when she was five she's a great dancer'.
'I think it's nice to have an interest outside school'.
'Harmony loves it gives me an hour to myself she's a good kid I'm really lucky' 'do you work?'.

'Part time shop work I finish at two so I can collect her from school will Kaleigh be wanting to come over?'.
'I don't know if she's emotionally ready she's really shy you know something like this it might be too much'.
'I know in the conversation we had she was really interested to find out what happened to Harmony'.
'Kaleigh was upset that she was taken away at a few weeks old' 'oh right' 'I got the impression'.
'That she wanted to give her up from social services' 'no'.
'She didn't have a choice it was for the best she wouldn't have been able to cope with a baby'.
'It was a decision made by Aunt Sue and Shaun her husband they brought her up my mum was an alcoholic'.
'And a drug addict she's been clean for years but they never let her see Kaleigh supervised visits'.
'By the time Kaleigh was six she was clean but she didn't get custody till she was fifteen joint custody'.
'With Aunt Hilary' 'that's a long time not to see Kaleigh' 'yeah Shaun he wasn't very nice to Kaleigh'.
'He used to call her names thick stupid a waste of space he was a horrible man'.
'They only got custody because they lived in a nice area'.
'When she was fifteen they went to Spain to open a bar they took their son Steven left Kaleigh'.
'She didn't know till she came home from school'.
'That's awful' 'mum and Hilary getting custody was the best thing that ever happened' 'I'm glad I met you Polly'.

'Now I have some background on Kaleigh' 'I'm glad'.
'I could help' 'I'm dreading telling Harmony she's adopted I know I have to do it but it'll be hard'.
'Do you know what you're gonna say?' 'just things'.
'That I'm not her real mum but I am in every other way'.
'If you just say her mum was too young when she had her that she loved her' 'good idea'.
'But she couldn't look after her so you did and you love her' 'thanks Polly I need to do it soon'.
'Before she starts secondary school I'd hate for her to find out when she's a teenager'.
'And then her school work suffers she goes off the rails'.
'If I get it done then they'll be no secrets between us'.
'I'm sure it won't be as bad as you think can I ask you a favour? you can say no if you want'.
'I was wondering if you have a photo of Harmony'.
'Of course you can have one' 'are you sure?' 'yes'.
'As luck would have it I got some extras done the other day it's so I can show Kaleigh' 'I'll go get them'.
Polly knew her sister would love to see a photo of her daughter 'here you go' 'thanks'.
Vanya handed her one A5 photo and one small one.
'Nice photo' 'I get a professional one done every year'.
They heard the doorbell ring as Vanya's friend brought Harmony round 'have a good time?' 'yeah'.
'I've got a friend round you remember Polly' 'yeah' 'hi'.
Polly though how pretty she looked just like Kaleigh.

With darker hair she was going to enjoy getting to know her niece Harmony seemed really sweet.
She couldn't wait to tell Kaleigh all the gossip the next day Polly asked her dad to make sure Sarah was out the house.
So she could chat to Kaleigh alone just the two of them.
Sarah went into town shopping with a friend as Polly had her opportunity to talk to her sister alone.
'Do you know mum's gone out so I can talk to you'.
'I've got some exciting news' 'what is it?' 'you remember a while ago when we chatted about your daughter'.
'How upset you were when you had to give her away'.
'How you didn't think that she'd want to know you'.
'Yeah' 'I've found her' Kaleigh smiled 'where is she?'.
'Still in Liverpool it's a nice area where she lives'.
'I got an address off my old social worker so I thought I'd just see where she lived'.
'This old woman says are you looking for Vanya she's round the corner at the park I never said who I was'.
'I was curious I went to the park I waited I was looking for a girl who might look a bit like you'.
'Strawberry blonde hair anyway this woman recognises me she's with this girl brown curly hair pale skin'.
'She says her name is Harmony she's ten that she's adopted because she couldn't have kids we get chatting'.
'She says she has mild dyslexia it had to be her'.
'I asked mum to come with me a week later to the park'.
'She told me not to see Vanya again that she'd be angry'.

'If she knew who we were she gave me her mobile number mum said she might be upset'.
'Think we were trying to take Harmony away that
I shouldn't see her again' 'did you?' 'course I did'.
'Mum can't tell me what to do I saw Vanya in town I had to tell her who I was' 'what did she say?'.
'She was alright about it I was surprised all she knew about the adoption was you were a teen mum'.
'She was grateful to get some background information'.
'Vanya's lovely I went round her house' 'does she look like me?' 'yeah thank god she doesn't look like you know who'.
'Apart from having brown curly hair and she's got
your face' 'does she know about Shaun?' 'no'.
'Vanya thinks it was some lad when you were thirteen'.
'It's best we keep it a secret agreed' 'yeah' 'Harmony's
not to blame or you I've got a photo of her'.
'If you wanna see' Polly showed Kaleigh a photo.
'Isn't she pretty' Polly could see how happy Kaleigh was 'you'll be looking at that photo all day long now'.
'What's she like?' 'she seems really sweet shy like you'.
'Harmony goes to dance classes does tap she's really good Vanya says there must be a dance gene in the family'.
'Would you do me a favour' 'anything' 'don't say anything to mum about me seeing Vanya again I'll talk to mum'.

'Not today keep the photo somewhere safe' 'Susie I won't say anything about Vanya' her dad said.
'But you need to talk to your mum' 'ok dad thanks for helping us give us a chance to chat' 'anytime'.
'Can I look at the photo?' Polly showed her dad.
'She's pretty' 'yeah she's gorgeous' at that moment Sarah returned Simon put the photo in a book.
'How's everyone?' 'great' 'got pizza for tonight'.
'It's cold out there' 'I can imagine' Polly said acting normal that evening they went out to see a show.
They had a great time Polly was happy she enjoyed spending time with her sister.
The next morning she was in good spirits 'you're in a good mood today' Sarah asked 'yeah I am'.
'I wonder why would this have anything to do with Vanya?' 'what do you mean?' 'you're phone went off'.
'The other night' 'spying on me!' 'no alright I read some texts looks like you two are getting close'.
'She's a nice person' 'this won't end well Susie'.
'When Vanya decides she doesn't want her birth mother and family involved' 'we're not getting involved!'.
'It's not like we're on her doorstep every day'.
'I keep a distance I don't want Vanya thinking we're trying to take her away I'm her Aunt!'.

'What if one day Vanya decides she doesn't want you coming round anymore' 'she won't!'.
'How do you know six months a year from now she might change her mind and you'll be hurt'.
'I'm trying to protect you' 'I don't need protecting!'.
'Everything's ok at least I'm taking an interest'.
'Don't come crying to me! when it all ends in tears!'.
'I won't!' Polly was angry at her mum she didn't care what she thought she loved her niece and liked Vanya.
As a friend and knew how happy Kaleigh was at seeing her photo why couldn't her mum be more understanding.
That afternoon Polly decided to do some housework.
It was a cold April afternoon her dad had gone out to see a friend in town she heard the door open 'mum'.
She looked angry 'what is it?' 'so you didn't think to mention Kaleigh had been raped then!'.
'I was gonna tell you' 'when?' 'I never got round to it'.
'I thought it was some lad all the time it was my sister's husband he raped my little girl'.
'Do you know how that feels! 'I'm sorry I was protecting you we all were we knew how upset you'd be' 'who's we?'.
'Me Hilary Maggie' 'who else knows?' 'Stacey I'm sorry'.
'Everyone except me' 'I meant to tell you it was never the right time I've only just found out myself'.

'You couldn't tell me my daughter had been raped'. 'Do you know how much I love Kaleigh' 'you think I don't!' 'how long have you known?' 'a while'. 'Everyone knew! except me!' 'Maggie's his daughter'. 'She knew what he was like' 'I like Maggie but she's not family' 'she is to me!' 'I'm her mum Kaleigh is my world'. 'I love that girl I'd die for her to think you lied about this and Stacey! Maggie even my own sister'. 'Do you know how that makes me feel! I wonder what Vanya will think when she finds out who the father is!'. 'She won't' 'you better hope not!' 'you can't blame this on me!' 'I can some bastard raped my little girl'. 'The most precious thing in the world to me you never told me! instead you're cosying up to Vanya'. 'Who's daughter was a product of...' 'no mum this had nothing to do with him!' 'how can you say that!'. 'Harmony's an innocent little girl who needs to be loved I'm not gonna stop loving her'. 'Because of who her dad is Kaleigh won't stop caring for her thinking about her cause you say so!'. 'Has Kaleigh met her?' 'not yet' 'good she's not going to!' 'mum!' 'no she doesn't need all this I look out for her'. 'Make sure she's ok and you wonder why we don't get on'. 'When you do things like this! I'm not happy Polly!'.

'That's my daughter who's been sexually abused!'.
'I know!' 'by my sister's husband and you never told me do you know how that makes me feel!' 'mum it's not fair!'.
'No it's not fair me being lied to by my family!'.
'Where is Kaleigh?' 'in the garden' 'good go upstairs'.
'I need a chat with my daughter now alone!'.
Polly had never felt more unloved by her own mum.
Or unwanted by the woman who was supposed to love her unconditionally.
Who was now subconsciously trying to blame her for her sister being sexually abused by Shaun.
When she'd first met up with her mum as an adult they'd been close now they were distant.
Their love hate relationship was now more hate.
That evening Polly cried in her pillow she now hated her.
She'd referred to Kaleigh as her little girl and her daughter the words 'you know how much I love Kaleigh'.
And 'Kaleigh is my world' in her head it was so hurtful.
Yes Kaleigh had mild learning difficulties but did it mean she shouldn't be loved ignored forgotten about.
Polly knew deep down Kaleigh was her mum's favourite her youngest daughter that they'd always been close.
And she was closer to her dad did that mean she shouldn't be loved too?

Kaleigh would never answer back to her mum she was the perfect daughter Polly would tell her mum her opinion.
If she didn't agree with it their personalities clashed her mum saw things differently in black and white.
Her mum always wanted to know the gossip where as she liked to be more tactful she'd seen her mum's true colours.
What she was really like and didn't even want to ask her if she loved her Polly knew what the answer would be.
How had their relationship gotten so bad? even worse she wanted to stop Kaleigh meeting Harmony.
Didn't she have a right to meet her own daughter.
The next morning things were playing on her mind Sarah even called her Polly which she rarely did.
It was always Susan or Susie she decided not to dwell on their row which was hard she left for London.

Las Vegas wedding

So she could see Maggie she told Kaleigh she'd be back soon she also had some good news.
She'd finally gotten pregnant on her third attempt.
Of course she and Margie were happy she needed something to take her mind off things.
Polly didn't want anyone finding out before she was three months gone or at least ten weeks.
She especially didn't want her mum coming round saying she was sorry about their row.
Or buying baby clothes before the scan this was her time to enjoy her happy news and being with Margie at home.
It was a rainy day in Ireland as Corey received a phone call from Steve.
'I feel like you know we had unfinished business'.
'I wanted to call you I thought you might be busy' 'no'.
'You should have called I thought I'd done something wrong' 'no' 'that kiss we had in Scotland'.
'I thought it might not mean anything that you'd have a girl back home waiting for you' 'no there's no-one else'.
'You always assume that I go on all these dates with different women I actually enjoy my own company'.
'You want the truth' 'yes' 'there's been no-one else'.

'Since our relationship no-one serious just a few dates you know why because no-one will compare to you'.
'I have loved you ever since we did I Love Paris together'.
'I tried to tell you so many times I love you' 'this is so hard for me for twenty years I've been a lesbian'.
'I have been happy most of the time I've done gay bars I've loved every part of gay culture'.
'I've been proud of who I am me falling for you I didn't know how to feel that's why I ended our relationship'.
'I still fancy lust after women in magazines on TV'.
'In the street I can't change who I am' 'I'm not asking you to I would never ask you to change who you are'.
'I love you please be my girlfriend or fiancé'.
'Please marry me you can still have women on the side'.
'I don't care I've never loved anyone like I love you'.
'Please don't make me wait another five years to kiss or hold you or have a relationship with you' 'ok'.
'Even though I'm gay and I don't fancy men'.
'I fancy you Steve there's something about you'.
'I hate being unhappy I want you in my life ever since Scotland I haven't stopped thinking about you'.
'That kiss dreaming I could do it all again so yes I accept your proposal' 'really!' 'yes' 'you've made me so happy'.
Gay or not Corey knew she was in love with Steve.

A few days later he came to see her in Ireland she'd never felt so alive for days they were in bliss.
Until Daniel returned from London he announced he was coming over Corey had to tell Steve to stay away.
From the house she texted him later that evening to come back Corey knew her brother wouldn't be happy.
If he found out she decided to take a trip to Las Vegas she needed to get away from everything.
Her mum said she would look after Marie and Susan Corey invited all her band mates to Vegas Kitty, Daniel, Mike and Louie.
If she didn't invite Daniel he would wouldn't be happy.
They could all spend some quality time together relaxing and having fun it would be good to get away.
They went to all the bars visited a strip club with plus sized women and of course went on the roulette machines.
For a bit of gambling Corey was also secretly planning to marry Steve if she could get away from everyone.
She'd planned to meet him outside the Palm Springs hotel alone she had a few hours to kill.
Corey had just finished doing her make-up for the evening when Kitty insisted they go out for some drinks.
If she said no it would be obvious she was up to something she had two drinks before they saw a cabaret show.

Having a drink would relax her Corey hoped the show wouldn't go on too long it was an hour and a half.
She was meeting Steve at 10.30pm she was wearing a blue dress and a beret and thought she looked nice.
They headed back to the hotel Corey checked she looked ok 'listen I need to go talk to Louie I'll be back'.
'In ten minutes' 'ok darling see you in a bit'.
Corey left quickly as she made her way outside.
She panicked as she saw her brother she hid behind a tree he passed by with Mike as she arrived at the Palms Hotel.
Steve wasn't there she was only two minutes late 'hey'.
'Steve I thought I'd missed you' 'never you look lovely'.
'How could I miss marrying the love of my life' they made their way to the chapel together inside was an Elvis.
And Kieran who were witnesses Steve presented Corey with a gold ring with a blue sapphire her favourite.
They were married she felt happy that Steve would look after her 'now you may kiss the bride'.
As they kissed it felt great of course she was sad that she had to hide who she was marrying.
But she'd done the big white wedding before.
'Congratulations' 'thanks Kieran that was fun I love Elvis' 'he was great' 'you're my wife now'.
'I know I'm so lucky' Steve kissed her it felt amazing.

'What do you say we have a few drinks to celebrate'.
Kieran suggested 'sounds great' they hit the bars.
As they had a few drinks Corey was by now very tipsy
around midnight she returned to her hotel room.
After saying goodnight to Steve and Kieran 'I wondered
where you went' Kitty said 'I'm grand I am drunk'.
'Who did you go out with?' 'Steve and Kieran'.
'Let me make you a cup of tea sober you up' 'I'm fine'.
'Cor' 'listen I have some mineral water at least you had
a good time' 'oh yes I did' Kitty got out her pyjamas.
As she helped her get ready for bed she soon fell asleep as
Corey woke the next day she was happy she had breakfast.
Pretending like nothing happened that morning they all
took a walk around Las Vegas after lunch Daniel saw her.
As she sat near the waterfalls 'what have you done!'.
'What do you mean?' 'all morning I've been getting
messages from people you married him'.
'You married Steve here in Las Vegas last night?' 'yes'.
'I wondered where you went to now I know'.
'It just happened' 'Cor you got married' Kitty said.
'You were really drunk when you came back to our hotel
room last night do you remember?' 'vaguely'.
'I even had to put you to bed' 'this is great!'.

'You were intoxicated' Daniel said 'I had a few drinks'.
'More than a few it's ok we can get it annulled'.
Daniel said 'Britney did it should be easy we'll find out who does marriages you researched marriage laws'.
'For Polly that time when she got forced to marry Natalie you said yourself you can say it was fraud'.
'That you were drunk you didn't know what you were doing' Kitty said 'she's right it'll be fine' 'ok'.
'If you think I can get it annulled how did you find out?'.
'It's all over Twitter a British tourist saw you get married' 'oh great!' 'it's ok you weren't thinking straight
'We'll sort it' Daniel said 'if I see Steve I'll kill him' 'no'.
'He got you drunk then you got married' Kitty said 'ok'.
'I'll get it annulled and it'll be fine' inside Corey felt sad she'd wanted to marry Steve more than anything.
But she'd been unlucky enough to be spotted by a tourist she had no choice but to get it annulled.
The lesbian community would never forgive her if they knew she loved a man.
A large part of her fan base were other lesbians.
Corey wrote on Twitter 'last night got married to a friend while drunk not a good idea' #Vegas.
Daniel also wrote 'my sister will be getting her marriage annulled what happens in Vegas stays in Vegas'.

Corey went to see Steve 'hey gorgeous' 'listen if you see my brother stay out of his way he's not happy'.
'Someone saw us get married it's all over the internet'.
'Is that a bad thing at least now we can be open and honest about things' 'no you don't get it how Daniel is'.
'Tell him where to go' 'I'm sorry I have to get our marriage annulled' 'why?' 'because I just do'.
'I'm really sorry!' 'no this isn't happening!' 'I'm sorry'.
'If I hurt you Steve' 'no you told me I'm the only man you ever loved' 'you are you know that' 'don't do this!'.
'I have to' 'no you don't' 'I do!' 'because of your brother'.
'Different reasons' 'you do that!' 'Steve I'm sorry'.
'Your brother doesn't want us to be happy want his own sister to be happy! you're an adult'.
'You can do what you want so we get married and it means nothing!' 'I was happy last night when we got married'.
'Now you're not' 'I have no choice my brother management whoever it's for the best'.
'If that's how you feel!' 'you're a good friend to me'.
'You know that' 'you always say that I didn't care that you like women about your sexuality'.
'We could have an open marriage I would have loved you you know that' 'I'm sorry I've upset you'.
'I'm going back to L.A' 'please don't be angry at me'.

'How can I not be!' 'please forgive me' 'I'll try'.
Corey could see how hurt Steve was disappointed angry she hated herself most of all she hated Daniel.
If it wasn't for his jealousy over Steve her brief moment of happiness ruined by her own brother.
When she got back to Dublin Corey felt sad she tried not to dwell on things her mum comforted her.
Telling her that it was ok that everyone makes mistakes the problem was Steve wasn't a mistake.
He would have made her happy after she'd been unhappy for so long they'd always been good friends.
When they'd kissed in Scotland and the hotel room in Las Vegas it had been special she'd thought of Steve.
Played out romantic scenarios in her head now she'd ruined everything.
He'd probably never want to speak to her again.
That evening her brother called to say he was coming round she didn't really want to see him.
Corey was still angry at him for ruining things with Steve.
When he turned up he was two hours late and smelled of alcohol and had been drinking she reluctantly let him in.
'Had a drinking session' 'maybe' 'glass of orange'.
'To sober up' 'why not?' Daniel sat down on the sofa.

As she poured them some juice 'you need to find a nice girl instead of spending Friday nights alone'.
'I have been married before' 'I know he's clearly just wanting to get into your knickers' 'no he's not!'.
'You are really stupid if you think he's not'
'I know your drunk don't call me stupid!'.
'You were drunker than I am when you married him'.
'Yes I really like him' 'no please tell me your joking!'.
'That wedding wasn't real' 'it was real! the only reason I had it annulled was because a British tourist found out'.
'And my career would have been affected if my lesbian fans found out'.

Broken families

'I knew something was going on when we were in
New York!' Daniel had sobered up and was angry.
'We only kissed' 'when?' 'in Scotland lesbian or not
I really like him' 'rubbish! he's using you!'.
'Why would he do that?' 'his career was in decline before
he met you!' 'so what's that go to do with anything!'.
'He needs you to make money that's why he asked you to
do that film Neighbours From Hell' 'you're just jealous'.
'Why would I be jealous of him!' 'you tell me!'.
'Because we're close so you've always been the only man
in my life well not anymore!'.
'You end your relationship with him now!' 'I don't need to
you just ended it! by making me end my marriage'.
'For your own good!' 'how is it for my own good!'.
'To stop you making another mistake!' 'Steve's not a
mistake! I love him' 'how can you!' 'I love him!'.
Daniel smacked her across the face Corey was shocked.
'You go anywhere near him!' 'you can't stop me!'.
'I'm gonna talk to him we're gonna have a
proper relationship' 'you're not! I'll make sure of it!'.
'Go on then!' he grabbed her as he smacked her in the
face she was instantly transported to her childhood.

And teenage years and their dad 'get out!' 'not till you promise me you won't see him again!'.
'If it's what you want' 'I said promise' 'I won't see him again' 'good!' Daniel left as Corey started shaking.
Her heart beating as she cried for over an hour.
On the sofa alone in a distressed state she was shocked.
Her own brother had always loved and protected her despite being a year older.
She'd always felt like he was the older one Corey never thought she'd see the day when her brother was violent.
As their father had been the next day she made plans to go to London she was worried in case he came back again.
Drunk and angry she thought she could see Lucy her old friend from the gay scene and Polly.
Corey checked into a hotel still shaken up about what had happened the next day she met up with Polly and Margie.
In town as she pretended everything was ok as she covered up her bruised eye with heavy foundation.
And smoky blue eyeshadow 'let's go clubbing tonight' Polly suggested 'sounds good'.
'We could go to Candies or Shockwaves just like old times' 'yeah ok sounds great.
Corey felt better being with Polly and Margie she hoped they wouldn't notice that she wasn't herself.

Margie was back at her old job as a beauty therapist in Soho her old boss Julie had left.
And she was enjoying work Polly had to attend a meeting about Britain's Got Talent she was due to start as a judge.
She was excited about her new role on the panel she was only a few weeks pregnant so it wouldn't be an issue.
Margie was going to give Corey a massage she hoped it would make her feel better as Corey took off her top.
She knew she was being quieter than usual 'can I ask what happened with the wedding? in Las Vegas' 'yeah tell me'.
'I had a few drinks Steve's a good friend it was a mistake'.
'I was a bit tipsy' 'we've all done things we regret'.
'I thought you'd reverted' 'no we had a relationship once'.
'But I went back to women' 'well it could happen to anyone getting drunk getting married in Las Vegas'.
'If you want my opinion I hate the idea it might seem like fun but if I'm getting married I want to do it properly'.
'I agree' Corey felt like Margie could read her mind .
'How's your brother?' 'I...I don't know' Corey could feel herself shaking 'are you ok?' 'I will be'.
'Tell me what's wrong?' 'it's nothing really' 'let me thread your eyebrows I promised last time'.
'Do you need me to take my eyeshadow off?'
'just the top part I had some eye make-up wipes'.

'Shall I do it?' 'yeah ok' Margie wiped off her eye make-up Corey knew she'd ask what the bruising was from.
'What's that red mark from? don't say nothing'.
'A man broke into my house he punched me'.
'That's terrible' 'I know' 'do you know who it was?' 'no'.
'Have you reported it?' 'it's fine' 'no it's not he might attack other people did he steal anything?' 'I don't know'.
'Darling you're shaking' 'I know' 'please tell the police'.
'Maybe' Margie threaded her eyebrows she felt better.
She hated having to lie about things that evening before they went out Margie decided to talk to Polly about Corey.
'Listen has Corey told you anything that she was attacked' 'no you're joking!' 'some man came into her house'.
'Punched her in the eye' 'that's awful' 'she won't go to the police I made her take her make-up off'.
'She had this bruise a red and blue mark she's really shaken up she was actually shaking'.
'As she told me the story' 'I hope she's ok' 'she needs to report whoever it is' 'I'm ready' 'Cor'.
'Margie told me what happened please tell the police'.
'Are you ok?' 'yeah I just want to forget about it'.
'What if he does it again' 'I'll be ok' 'I'm just worried'.
'That you won't be at least you'll have Dan around'.

'I promise it won't happen again I won't put myself in that situation' 'you've always got us to talk to' 'thanks'.
'Let's go out have a good time' Polly and Margie were worried about Corey but couldn't do anything.
They had a good night out clubbing Corey only stayed a few days in London returning to Dublin.
She hoped she wouldn't have to see her brother again.
No chance as he insisted on cooking her a meal to apologise she didn't see why not if he was genuinely sorry.
They cooked together it was nice as Corey went to wash her hands in the bathroom she returned.
Daniel had an angry look on his face 'I need to talk to you alone upstairs' 'Dougie watch the pan'.
'If it bubbles too much turn it down one minute'.
Corey was curious as to why her brother needed to talk to her 'what's up?' 'come here' she followed him.
Into her bedroom as he shut the door 'do you think I'm stupid!' 'what do you mean?' 'Steve'.
'Look at these texts!' 'give me my phone!' 'look at this one it's ok I forgive you for getting our marriage annulled'.
'I'll always love you and can't wait to see you again'.
'Hold you in my arms and show you how much I love you and the sent messages Steve I'm so sorry'.

'Please forgive me I don't know what I'd do without you in my life so this is a proper romance now' 'yes'.
'We want to have a relationship!' 'does this include sex?'.
'Maybe' 'so you're straight now' 'no I still like women'.
'But I'll be having a relationship with a man' 'so you're bi' 'maybe' 'really you never took up my advances!'.
'You're my brother you know your feelings towards me are wrong I thought we'd talked about this before'.
'That our relationship was back to being what it should be' 'maybe I want to get into your bed too!'.
Daniel pushed her 'we'll see how straight you are!'.
As he lay on top of her on the bed she felt scared 'no!'.
He put his hand over her mouth so she couldn't shout or scream he undid the zip on her trousers.
She tried to fight him 'Carol's here' Douglas shouted.
*As Daniel removed his hand from her mouth 'f**k you'.*
'And that American bastard!' he got up.
As he went downstairs Corey was in shock her heart beating would her own brother have raped her?.
She was shaking as she went to the bathroom.
Trying to compose herself she reapplied some lipstick.
As she went downstairs to see Carol she'd have to pretend everything was ok 'Corey come here' she hugged her.

It felt so good she held her tighter than usual 'love you'.
'It's so good to see you' 'I hope you don't mind me turning up like this' 'no where's John?' 'he's at a friends house'.
'We're having a stir fry' 'sounds good are you ok?' 'yes why?' 'Polly said you were broken into by a man'.
'On Facebook that some man punched you in the face'.
'It's fine I'm ok' 'you live here alone do you want me to move in for a while?' 'she's ok she's got me' Daniel said.
'I know I just worry how did this man get in?'.
'I left the door open it was a one off stupid mistake'.
'Don't worry it could happen to anyone' 'oh I've forgotten I have to pick up Connor I'll be back soon'.
'Ten minutes' Corey didn't want to be left alone with her brother now she knew he was a potential rapist.
She stirred the pan shaken up 'ready yet?' Douglas asked.
'Just a moment' Corey set the table for Carol's return.
'I'll do that' Daniel said 'I want you nowhere near me!'.
'I never meant to upset you' Corey didn't reply not wanting Douglas to find out what happened.
Carol soon returned as they drank wine anything to help her forget things that her brother had tried to rape her.
After dinner Corey decided to take Carol up on her offer of going home.
She couldn't spend the night in her own house.

And what if Daniel tried to attack her again.
'Really you don't need to go' 'no I do' 'what's this about?' 'we had a row' Daniel explained 'more than a row!'.
'Nothing we can't work out between us' 'I want you gone by tomorrow afternoon when I come home'.
'Anything you want' 'I'll be off now have a good evening'.
As Corey shut the door she felt relieved to be away from her brother 'Corey what was that all about?'.
'I can't be alone in the house with him tonight'.
'What's wrong? you don't seem yourself' Corey began to cry 'darling it's ok had he said something to upset you?'.
'Don't worry come round to mine we'll have a chat'.
As Corey arrived at Carol's John was there to greet them.
'What's wrong?' 'me and Corey need to have a chat alone' 'ok I'll be in the other room'.
After a few minutes Corey calmed down her mum comforted her 'tell me what's wrong' 'it's Daniel'.
'What's he done?' 'he has feelings for me that he shouldn't' Carol didn't say anything.
She knew what Corey meant but was surprised at her confession Corey could have lied to her mother.
She would have done years ago but lying for her brother wasn't the right thing to do anymore.
'Are you saying what I think you're saying' 'yes'.

'He kissed me more than a peck on the lips'.
'You know what I'm saying' 'how long has he...?'.
'Had these feelings for?' 'years I told him I said
a few years ago how I felt'.
'That our relationship was brother and sister I told a
counsellor in New York I felt so ashamed' 'no Corey'.
'You've got nothing to be ashamed of he upset you tell me
what happened' 'he forced himself on top of me'.
'He tried to have sex with you' 'I was scared he's
never done anything like that before'.
'It was like he was another person I didn't know anymore'.
'I don't know if he would have done anything to me'.
'I couldn't stay in the house' 'it's ok you stay here with me'.
'I've asked him to leave' 'he better or I'll be having words
with him that bruise near your eye was that him?' 'yes'.
'He's jealous of my relationship with Steve' 'no man
should ever hit a woman especially not his own sister'.
'He's not usually like this' 'please don't make excuses'.
'I'm not but he's my brother we grew up together'.
'We both had physical abuse from our father we had
no-one else we never told anyone'.
'In case we were put into care and separated he was the
only person who understood me'.

'What I was going through as a child' 'I understand'.
'But that's still no excuse for what he tried to do his feelings are wrong it's incest' 'I know that'.
'When did you first realise he had feelings for you?'.
'I was nineteen I came home to visit Dublin after moving to London he kissed me on the lips passionately'.
'I thought it was weird strange I thought he was just happy to see me then he did it again two years later'.
'We did X Factor he came into the dressing room'.
'Over the years it would be little things like him trying to put his hand where he shouldn't round my waist'.
'I knew how Daniel felt about me then one time I was twenty eight he kissed me I kissed him back'.
'It wasn't even that I had feelings for him I don't'.
'It was a comfort thing because I felt alone upset about splitting up with Polly' 'he took advantage of you'.
'I'm angry at myself for kissing him back I feel like it made him have stronger feelings for me'.
'I just want us to have a normal relationship not like this'.
'I thought we did but at the back of my mind it's like if I touch him by accident'.
'It will make him have more inappropriate feelings for me I love him as my brother nothing else'.
'He tried to rape you your own brother' 'but did he?'.

'He was on top of me angry having a go at me'.
'Because I got a text from Steve then you came round I don't know would have happened if you hadn't'.
'I'm not sticking up for him but I don't know if he would have or not was he just angry at me'.
'I just don't want to be around him at the moment'.
'I'm happy you told me about things I will look after you make sure you're ok you know how much I love you'.
Corey loved her mum she also felt better for telling her everything the truth about her life.
And screwed up relationship with Daniel a few days later she decided to try and block out what had happened.
With her brother she still felt scared of him he'd been angry in Las Vegas over Steve.
But Corey refused to let go of the idea of having a relationship with him he could make her happy.
Steve loved her she knew he did he didn't mind that she still fancied women he was a good friend.
Corey returned to London to audition for a film called Fat Women about a slimming group.
She really wanted the role the character was in an abusive relationship and battling her sexuality.
It seemed like art imitating life her own brother hitting her and dealing with the fact she could be bi-sexual.

Corey thought she'd done a good audition.
But had no idea whether she'd got it that evening she went to see Polly and Margie with her mum.
Who had come along knowing how vulnerable she felt.
They greeted them 'come in darling' 'hi Carol' Polly said.
'Hi Polly' 'cup of tea?' 'we'd love one' Corey was hoping Polly wouldn't notice anything was wrong.
'Are you ok after that man breaking in?' Polly asked.
'I'm grand' 'I'd be scared if it was me' Polly said.
'Really I'm ok' 'back in a minute' Polly said going to make the tea 'what's this about someone breaking in?'.
Polly brought in the tea 'shortbread homemade'.
'Looks nice' 'have you reported that guy yet?' Polly asked 'no' 'you need to in case he attacks someone else'.
'He won't' 'how do you know he might' 'please shut up about it ok!' Corey snapped 'I'm sorry'.
'I was only trying to be a friend' 'Corey's not herself'.
'I'm sorry I never meant to have a go at you'.
'Why don't you tell Polly the truth about what happened'.
'I can't' 'I won't let you lie for him' 'who? tell me'.
'I promise it won't go any further' 'Daniel hit Corey in the face and that's the truth' 'why?' 'he's jealous'.
'Of my friendship with Steve always has been' 'Cor'.

'It's fine it was a one off ok he's always been the only man in my life' 'you're just mates' 'of course'.
'So there was no break in you made it up to cover for him' 'yes he's been angry lately I don't know why'.
'You should never hit a woman' 'I know ok'.
'Sounds like there's something going on in his life to make him behave like that he's always been a good friend to me'.
'Has he apologised?' 'no not yet' 'he should have' just then Christian arrived 'hey darling' 'hi everyone'.
'I'm not interrupting anything?' 'no the more the merrier'.
'Tea and shortbread' Polly asked 'yes please' 'so you're over from Ireland with Corey' Christian asked Carol 'yes'.
'I'm looking out for her she's not been herself' 'Polly told me what happened I'm sorry' 'it's ok' Corey said.
'I'm actually I'm here because I auditioned for a film'.
'Oh great' 'it's called Fat Women about a slimming group' 'sounds great I hope I get it' Polly returned with the tea.
'Looks nice I brought some of that champagne you like' 'oh great do you mind if I have it another night?'.
'No course not' 'thanks' Polly couldn't risk news of her pregnancy getting out so early.
And if she drank alcohol it might be bad for the baby.
If she refused they'd wonder why 'Christian's sweet like that bringing me round gifts it was a box of Milk Tray'.

'Last time I saw him' 'that's nice of him' 'you're the best brother in the world' 'I try to be'.

Corey couldn't help wishing she had a normal relationship with her brother like Polly and Christian did.

She still had Nicky she didn't dare tell her what was going on no-one would believe her.

Corey knew she'd have to talk to Daniel at some point.

Right now she just wanted to audition for the film a few days later she received some good news she'd got the role.

As she left her film meeting she felt good as she walked through the building she saw Christian 'hi how are you?'.

'Good I got the film role I wanted' 'well done' 'thanks'.

'What about you?' 'I came for a meeting about a role'.

'Would you like to go for a drink in a café?'

Christian asked 'I'd love to' Corey went with Christian.

As she ordered a chocolate milkshake 'so apart from going for film roles what else have you been up to?' 'not much'.

'The usual songwriting hanging out with the kids'.

'Sounds good I'm sorry to hear about what happened getting broken into' 'I never got broken into'.

'It was a cover my brother hit me I've told Polly now no point keeping it a secret' 'I'm sorry why?'.

'He's jealous of my friendship with Steve we've always been close he was always like my best friend'.

'It's like he doesn't want me speaking to anyone not another man' 'you should never hit a woman'.
'Well he didn't have a very good role model for a father growing up' 'even so it's wrong' 'I know'.
'If I ever found out anyone touched Maria or Polly'.
'I'd be really angry I know he's your brother why is he jealous? it's not like it's anything else going on'.
'It's more than friends I'm still a lesbian I like women'.
'But I like Steve we had a relationship before I went out with Stacey he said he loves me he's a good friend to me'.
'I can't tell anyone people wouldn't like it'.
'You won't tell anyone not even Polly or Stacey'.
'You have my word I promise' 'thanks I've never fancied men before I've always been with women'.
'There's something about Steve' 'sometimes it's about the person' 'Dan doesn't see it like that he was angry at me'.
'I've never seen him like that before I got married in Las Vegas Steve asked me so I said yes'.
'I had to get it annulled' 'it was real' 'I had two drinks'.
'I wasn't drunk management and Dan told me to get it annulled the lesbian community would never forgive me'.
'The whole thing went wrong getting married in Las Vegas it was a mistake I texted Steve to apologise'.

'Dan found the texts it wasn't good' 'I know it's not my place to say but you're brother should be ashamed'.
'Treating you like that' 'thanks for listening to my problems' 'it's ok'.
Corey realised she quite fancied Christian she really was bi-sexual what was happening to her?.
She recalled a night out clubbing with Lucy recently.
How angry she had been about one girl 'can you believe she's deflected to the other side'.
'I thought she was one of us you know a proper lesbian'.
'Thank god for you and Polly this bi-sexual rubbish please give me a break pick one side and stick to it'.
'Does bi-sexuality even exist' 'yes and no' Corey replied.
'I mean people can be attracted to different sexes at different times'.
'But you can't have a gay relationship alongside a heterosexual one unless you're having an affair'.
'You're either dating a man or a woman' 'you get it'.
'Exactly! my point' Lucy didn't exactly get what she was saying was she about to deflect to the other side?.
She hadn't fancied a girl since Stacey Corey told herself it was ok to fancy Steve or even Christian
Corey was grateful for Christian's company.
If she could focus on her new film everything would be ok.

She decided it would take her mind off things.
Polly was happy things were going well in her life.
She'd also been seeing a lot of Vanya they got on so well she'd also become attached to Harmony.
Polly loved her niece and hoped Kaleigh could meet her.
She knew her mum wouldn't approve if she knew how close they were she didn't care.
She knew she was doing the right thing Sarah had found out after seeing Vanya in town unknown to Polly.
And she wasn't happy about it one day while visiting Hilary in Liverpool she decided to go and see her.
As she rang the doorbell Vanya answered 'hello Sarah'.
'I'm sorry to just turn up like this' 'it's fine I wondered if you'd come round Polly spends so much time here'.
'I know I didn't realise you were so close'.
'You don't mind' 'it's not that I need to talk to you'.
'Of course a cup of tea?' 'I won't be staying'.
'Sounds serious' 'I only found out recently about Harmony that she existed I had no idea Polly was still visiting'.
'I told her not to is Harmony here?' 'no she's out'.
'At a dance class' 'good Polly told you the father was some lad from school it's not true' 'who is it?'.
'This is really hard to tell you the truth I hate to tell you'.

'I only found out myself recently it was a shock'.
'Kaleigh was raped by my sister's husband she wasn't even thirteen if I had a choice I wouldn't be telling you this'.
'I thought you should know the truth it's hard'.
'Kaleigh's my little girl it's hard for me to imagine…'.
'What she went through' 'I'm sorry I had no idea'.
'That's why I had to tell you Polly withheld this information from you and I understand why'.
'Because she wanted to get close to Harmony'.
'But she lied to you about who the dad was I thought you needed to know' 'I'm glad you told me the truth'.
'This changes things' 'I'm sorry no-one wants to hear news like that Shaun he's a horrible man'.
'I heard he recently got arrested for child sex offences'.
'At least that's something would he ever try and find Harmony?' 'no he wouldn't'.
'He doesn't even care about his first daughter trust me'.
'He won't have any interest in looking for you I'll let you deal with the news alone' 'thanks'.
'I appreciate you telling me it explains things' 'take it easy if you ever need any questions answered'.
'I know all I need to know thankyou bye Sarah'.
As Sarah left she knew she'd done the right thing no more lies she'd told Vanya the truth about Harmony.

That evening Polly received a text from Vanya she was in shock as she read it 'I know everything'.
'I appreciate your interest in Harmony'.
'But I think it's best you don't see her anymore please don't come to the house' *Polly was so upset.*
She knew only one thing would have changed how Vanya felt about her mum would have said something.
Told her not to have anything to do with her her mum had threatened to tell Vanya about Shaun before now she had.
She never thought she'd go through with it she must have there was no other explanation.
As to why Vanya would cut off contact with her.
How could her mum sink so low? she was obviously jealous she decided to text Vanya.
'I'm sorry you had to find out like this I was going to tell you please forgive me' *hours later she received nothing.*
Polly decided against going to see her mum she was so angry she didn't want to be anywhere near her.
And if she called her she would deny everything or say she had Kaleigh's best interests at heart.
A week later it was her uncle Sam's birthday party.
In Liverpool Polly was dreading it she would have to see her mum acting as if nothing had happened.
But she couldn't not go she was close to her uncle.

It would look bad if she didn't Polly selected a creme chiffon blouse she wasn't showing yet.
But she still didn't want to give anything away.
Margie was with her as they entered the house everyone said hello 'darling come here' Sam said hugging her.
'You look great tonight' 'thanks' Polly handed him her present 'lots of punch over there' 'we'll try some'.
'I'll be back in a minute' he said 'I don't know if I should have any punch' 'depends how strong it is' 'I won't risk it'.
'I'll have some then' Margie said Polly hadn't spoken to Margie about how angry she was at her mum.
Only saying that Vanya had stopped contacting her and she was upset about it.
That she suspected her mum had something to do with it.
Polly immediately clocked her mum and Kaleigh 'hey you two wondered where you were' Sarah said 'you look nice'.
Polly said noticing Kaleigh's dress her sister had on a cornflower blue dress with sapphire earrings 'nice dress'.
'Oh I brought it for her brand new the other day cost me a hundred pounds if you can't spoil your daughter'.
'Oh I agree' Margie said 'I always wanted a daughter'.
'Well I always wanted a son a gay son they always love their mums me and Kaleigh we've got matching outfits'.

'Both wearing blue' 'how nice seems I never got the memo if you'll excuse me I'm gonna see some family members'.
'Who actually care about me' 'Susie don't be like that'.
'I'm sure your mum never meant it the way it sounded'.
'Yeah she did she doesn't love me she only loves Kaleigh'.
'Not me' 'it's not true' Margie said 'it is you weren't there that time when she had a go at me'.
'For not telling her Kaleigh was raped even though I only found out recently myself' 'you were protecting her'.
'Well I wish I hadn't bothered!' 'Polly' 'she's not as nice as you think she is and I know she told Vanya'.
'That Kaleigh was raped by Shaun and that's why she's stopped contacting me who knows what else she told her'.
'Mum threatened to tell Vanya the truth to stop me seeing Harmony!' 'why would she do that?'.
'Because she's jealous that I got close to Vanya'.
'You don't know my mum do you know we were actually close for a while when my Hollywood career took off'.
'I was like twenty one I wanted us to be close'.
'Have a proper relationship then eventually she just stopped loving me' 'mum's don't pick what kids they love'.
'Sometimes they do sometimes I'm not good enough and never will be' 'why don't you talk to your mum'.

'About things' 'look at them chatting away like I don't exist' 'hi Susie' 'dad' 'how are you?' 'I've been better'. 'What's up?' 'things' 'I don't think I'll be staying long'. 'Why not?' 'I need to talk to mum' 'she's over there'. 'I'll see you soon' Polly was glad her dad was there to calm the situation she was close to her uncle Sam. But was starting to wish she'd never come over. Kaleigh came over she noticed a silver bracelet. 'Did mum buy you that as well?' 'yeah have you heard anything about you know...' 'Harmony' 'yeah I have'. 'Mum ruined everything' 'how?' 'she told Vanya about Shaun now she wants nothing to do with me'. 'There's no chance of you seeing Harmony either'. 'You gave me a photo' 'ask mum about it' Kaleigh went over to talk to Sarah minutes later she walked over. An angry look on her face 'what the hell have you said to Kaleigh!' 'me!' 'yes you've upset her!'. 'More likely you have! I know exactly what you've done!'. 'What you said to Vanya why all of a sudden she's cut off contact with me for no reason' 'I did it for the best'. 'More likely you were jealous of my friendship with Vanya!' 'which was based on a lie'. 'How do you work that one out!' 'you never told her the truth!' 'so you thought you would out of spite!'.

'You want that girl growing up knowing who her father is'.
'She would never have known! I would never have said neither would Kaleigh' 'she would have found out'.
'How? she wouldn't if you hadn't said anything'.
'So everytime you see Harmony you don't think of him'.
'No because she looks more like Kaleigh' 'what about when she gets older starts asking questions'.
'That girl is a product of rape' Sarah said lowering her voice 'no this is not her fault she is innocent'.
'Stop referring to her as that girl she's my niece'.
'Please keep your voice down or do you want everyone finding out our private family business!'.
'I don't care anymore what you did was cruel and heartless!' 'what looking out for my daughter!'.
*'Yeah that's right your daughter who the f**k am I!'.*
'Some inconvenience!' by now people had started listening to their row 'Polly calm down please!' 'it's Susan'.
'Or have you forgotten my birth name I'm Polly Patterson celebrity not Susan Marie O'Malley your daughter'.
'Oh I forgot you've only got one daughter now Kaleigh'.
'I'm just an after thought sorry I'm not your youngest'.
'Or have special needs! it's alright just because I don't have special needs'.
'Doesn't mean I don't deserve any attention!'.

'You're showing yourself up now!' 'good! why don't you just admit you don't love me just tell everyone!'.

'You're being ridiculous!' 'by telling the truth you and Kaleigh going out on shopping trips'.

*'Where the f**k is my invite! oh I never get one! you and my sister so close! well you deserve each other!'.*

'Said your piece!' 'I've just begun!' 'here we go'.

'Embarrass yourself!' 'you know you're pathetic!'.

'Kaleigh's a twenty three year old woman you treat her like a sixteen year old kid you won't let her grow up'.

'She can't keep a house cook do anything for herself'.

'What would she do without Stacey!' 'leave Kaleigh alone if you're angry at me fine! don't bring her into this!'.

*'F**k you I'll make it easy for you! from now on you only have one daughter I don't exist!' 'stop acting jealous!'.*

'Yeah I am with good reason!' 'leave Sarah alone!'.

Luke said 'oh yeah course you think she's wonderful'.

'At least she was there for me when you were away all the time!' 'who pays for your computer games'.

'You've got no aspirations to do anything in life!'.

'At least I never took my clothes off for men!'.

'I've had it trying to please you apologise I can't do it anymore you can think what you want about me'.

'From now on! you know nothing about my life!'.

*'I know enough to know you were sleeping with your school teacher' 'one day I'll tell you about my teacher'. 'How he raped me when I was a teenager mum doesn't care either' 'come on don't have a go at Sarah'. Hilary said 'I know what everyone thinks of me f**k this family! Margie's my family now I don't need any of you!'. Polly walked out of the house as Margie followed. Polly cried as she comforted her 'come on darling let's go home you don't need the stress'.*

As they arrived at Polly's house Margie gave her a hug and a cup of tea she soon felt better. But upset after her row 'why doesn't she love Harmony like I do she's innocent in all this'. 'Mum had no reason to tell Vanya the truth' 'I know'. 'I won't stop loving her even if Vanya doesn't want to see me' 'she might change her mind' 'I doubt it'. 'If I was her I'd love someone like you around my daughter you'd be a good influence'. 'Vanya wouldn't see it like that' 'it'll be ok you just need a few days to get yourself together' 'I know'. 'In some ways I wish I'd never tracked her down'. 'Because I've just upset myself' 'it's ok tomorrow I'll give you a massage and a facial I'll make you feel better'.

'Thanks what would I do without you' Polly was glad Margie was there to make her feel better.
Although she didn't regret what she'd said to her mum.
Polly regretted slagging off her sister she loved Kaleigh.
It wasn't her fault she was her mum's favourite.
Or had mild learning difficulties now her sister would hate her think she didn't love her.
The next day as promised Margie gave her a massage and a facial before she put on her make-up.
She instantly felt better they decided to go shopping.
In Liverpool Polly also wanted to buy some clothes for when she got bigger Margie wanted to buy things.
For the baby Polly insisted she wait till the three month stage they had a good time together.
They felt solid as a couple like they'd been together forever Polly didn't know what she'd do without Margie.
As they walked around Polly spied a girl who looked like Harmony it was her as she looked over.
She was with some other adults Vanya wasn't there.
Polly knew she had to say hello 'it's Harmony'
'One minute' Harmony instantly recognised her 'Polly'.
'Not with your mum' 'no she's at work' 'are they your friends?' 'yeah are you gonna come round?' 'I can't'.

'Why?' 'your mum says I'm not allowed to come over anymore' 'I want you to'.

'I promise I will always be your friend'.

'And you can talk to me about anything' 'does that mean you won't come to the house anymore?' 'no'.

'But you know I'm a celebrity and sometimes I'm on TV'.

'Or I do a magazine interview you can always find out what I'm up to' 'I'll miss you' 'I'll miss you too'.

'You know we're friends forever' Polly was close to tears.

She'd built up a close relationship with Harmony.

Through all her visits it broke her heart to think she would never see her again 'Polly I'm Vanya's sister'.

'And she doesn't want you having anything to do with Harmony' 'I was just saying hello'.

'Harmony's got a family me Vanya her brother

I'd appreciate it if you stayed away'.

'There's no need to be nasty' Margie said 'I don't know who you are but if I see you near the house'.

'I'll call the police' 'that's a bit dramatic she was just being a friend' Margie said 'she has friends at school'.

'As far as we're concerned you're a famous celebrity'.

'Who used to visit her house we're her family she's legally adopted she has nothing to do with you or your sister'.

Polly watched as they walked away as she got out a tissue as tears fell down her face 'it's ok she was a bitch'.
'She was right it's my own fault I shouldn't have contacted her I've brought all this on myself' 'no darling'.
'Why do I feel like this about Harmony? what it is about her that makes me love her so much' 'she's a sweet girl'.
'And she's your niece' 'I can't see Harmony anymore'.
'Because she's not part of our family she is but we don't really know her' 'one day you will when she's sixteen'.
'And she leaves school she'll start asking questions who her mum is there's nothing Vanya can do'.
'No matter how much she loves Harmony tries to protect her it's human curiosity who's my mum'.
'What about the rest of my family' 'you can be honest tell her what you wanted to that you were never allowed'.
'You don't have to let her know about him she never has to find out' 'it hurts so much' 'I know'.
'But you've got no choice unless you want to get done for trespassing' 'you're right'.
'When she's older she'll know you love her'.
It still hurt Polly the whole situation.
But it was for the best she returned home as she relaxed.
After a stressful afternoon she listened to her answerphone.

She was surprised to hear a voice message from Louie.
'Hi it's Louie I'm sorry about everything call me darling'.
'I'd love for us to hang out sometime call me back'.
'It's Polly listen I'm not having a very good week'.
'My mum doesn't love me anymore and never has the same goes for my son it's not a great time for me at the moment'.
'I have Margie anyway I'll see you soon'.
She put the phone down 'forget about everyone it's just you and me tonight' 'I know I love you' 'love you too'.
They kissed for a moment everything was ok.
And Polly could forget about the fact she'd fallen out with her family she hated the drama.
At least she had something to look forward to her job.
On Britain's Got Talent for a few weeks she could have a laugh forget her problems.
As Polly arrived for her first day on the set of Britain's Got Talent she was nervous but excited.
She'd been asked to be a talent show judge before.
But had turned it down worried how she'd come across.
Or was too busy now she was free and always liked a new challenge.
In her dressing room were some bouquets of flowers one to her surprise was from Louie she read the note.

‘Good luck I know you’ll be amazing sorry about everything xxx’ she was touched.
Polly appreciated his gesture it was sweet.
And decided to go round to his house she was at war with her family at least she could see her friend.
As she knocked Louie opened ‘hi’ ‘Polly hello’.
‘I’m so sorry about things your mum’ ‘it’s alright'.
'Sorry I haven’t called lately’ 'it’s fine you’ve been busy’.
He hugged her holding her tight it felt good ‘come in'.
'I’ll make you a nice cup of tea’ she came in from the cold as they chatted ‘you look good as always’ Louie said.
‘Thanks for the flowers’ ‘I wanted to wish you luck’.
‘I appreciated it’ ‘I know you’ll be great so how’s everyone Kaleigh your mum?’ ‘I don’t know’.

'I'm not speaking to my family' 'I'm sorry to hear that'.
'What happened?' 'long story' 'you don't have to tell me'.
'But you know that saying a problem shared is a problem halved' 'trust me this is the worst row we've ever had'.
'Well I've never gotten on with my mum I always thought yours was ok' 'she is when she wants to be'.
'It's a personal family matter if I could tell you I would'.
'I don't want to speak to or see her ever again'.
'I understand at least you have Britain's Got Talent to focus on' 'and I've got Margie' 'how is she?' 'great'.
'We're still in love' 'that's so nice you're with someone who deserves you' 'yeah I am how's Angelica?' 'great'.
'She's twenty now can you believe it how fast time goes'.
'I know I have a twenty one year old son now'.
'How is he?' 'fine still obsessed with computer games'.
'And he still hates me' 'why?' 'he never forgave me for not being there because of my career'.
'It doesn't matter how good the films were not worth missing out spending time together'.
'I got bored on film sets they make you get up at six am then make you wait hours to do anything'.
'On the plus side I finished lots of games on the DS'.
'And wrote lots of song lyrics' 'you should use them'.
'I will anyway I've tried everything'.

'Luke wouldn't have the nice things he has all I get back is about me being called a slag'.
'Because I used to take my top off for men during my glamour modelling career'.
'I haven't got the energy to fight anymore' 'don't worry'.
'He'll come round' 'no Louie our relationships over'.
'I don't know him anymore' 'things will come ok in the end' 'no let him hate me he'll see when he's older'.
'Thinks he knows best' 'listen things are gonna be great in your career' 'yeah you're right'.
Polly decided to try and forget about her mum and Luke if they hated her it was their problem.
She went to the Britain's Got Talent auditions determined to prove herself a they were going all over the UK.
And stopping in Liverpool as Polly sat down that afternoon for auditions they had some ok acts on.
No-one that stood out she hoped that afternoon would get better she watched as a young girl walked on stage.
Wearing a dark green velvet coat she had mid-brown curly hair pale skin and was very pretty.
Polly suddenly realised it was Harmony 'hello'.
'What's your name?' 'Harmony Roberts' 'pretty name' one of the other judges said 'hi Harmony' Polly said.

'Hi' 'we know each other' 'how?' 'I used to go round her house for tea' 'can I come round for tea?'.
The other judge asked 'yeah' 'what are you gonna do?'.
'I'm gonna sing' 'what are you gonna sing for us?'.
Polly asked 'When You Wish Upon A Star' Polly hoped she'd be good it would be terrible if she wasn't.
As Harmony sang perfectly everyone cheered 'Harmony'.
'That was great Polly was your lucky charm' 'you did a great performance I love that song' Polly smiled happy.
She was proud of Harmony she left after being put through to the next round Polly felt on top of the world.
After thinking she'd never see Harmony again she believed things happened for a reason.
Vanya must have known she was a judge on the show it had been written about in all the magazines.
Maybe she was even backstage Polly decided not to check.
Later she was asked by one of the producers to go on the spin off show to talk to Harmony.
The last thing she needed was a row with Vanya getting out in the media all over the papers and magazines.
All she knew was that she'd had a good day and nothing could ruin her happiness at seeing Harmony again.
Corey was coming round to see her the next day she was doing some recording Polly would be joining her.

As Corey rang the doorbell she answered 'hey darling'.

'How are you?' Polly asked 'I'm alright you' 'good'.

'How's Britain's Got Talent going?' 'great fun'.

'I love all the acts when you watch on TV there's this one girl she's special you know' 'tell me'.

'You know Kaleigh what happened with Shaun' 'yeah'.

'How she had a baby and it was adopted well I contacted my old social worker I tracked her down'.

'I got her address I visited the park near her house I met her' 'Kaleigh's daughter?' 'yeah' 'I built up a friendship'.

'With her adoptive mum Vanya mum told me not to but I liked her she liked me' 'does she know you're her Aunt?'.

'She didn't at first then I told her who I was'.

'What happened?' 'Vanya didn't mind she was happy to get some background information on Kaleigh'.

'The circumstances of the adoption' 'she knows Kaleigh was raped?' 'she didn't till mum told her'.

'And ruined everything now she won't speak to me'.

'I'm sorry' 'there was no reason to do it she must have been jealous we're not speaking'.

'What does Kaleigh think?' 'she was happy I tracked her down I showed her a photo she never met Vanya'.

'Or Harmony' 'is that her name?' 'yeah she's gorgeous'.

'You'd love her I miss seeing her' 'you met her'.

'Lots of times I used to go round Vanya's for tea until mum ruined things after that she sent me a text'.
'Telling me to stay away from her it hurts I care about her she's my niece it's my own fault for contacting her'.
'I didn't know I'd feel like this I saw her in the shopping centre in Liverpool without Vanya'.
'Harmony said she missed me coming round it was hard explaining why I can't see her anymore'.
'Her mum's sister was there she told me to stay away'.
'And she was really nasty anyway I can't see her again'.
'Sounds unfair to me' 'guess what Harmony auditioned a few days ago for the show I was shocked'.
'I didn't know if she was with Vanya' 'was she any good?'.
'She was great she sang When You Wish Upon A Star'.
'Harmony's special you'd understand if you met her'.
'I wish I could explain to Vanya I can't the way things are'.
'It'll be ok' 'I don't know Cor I miss her but things happen for a reason'.
'That's why she auditioned for Britain's Got Talent' 'yeah' 'I'll show you I've got a photo' Polly returned with a photo of Harmony 'she's gorgeous' 'she's lovely'.
'Has Kaleigh met her?' 'not yet but she's seen her photo'.
'She'll love her when she sees her on TV if they show her I'm sure they will' Polly hoped they would.

She would be gutted if they didn't she was sure they would the next day Polly hung out with Corey.
Who'd brought their daughter's over she loved seeing them they were surprised when Daniel turned up.
At Polly's he apologised to Corey begging for forgiveness.
She forgave him partly because she didn't want anyone finding out about his behaviour Douglas looked up to him.
Kitty was in love with him if anyone found out it would destroy their perfect image of him.
And he had been drinking when he hit her that evening Stacey came round as everyone had a nice get together.
As they drank ate crackers chatting watching TV as Corey ventured upstairs Daniel followed her.
'Listen you know I am sorry about everything let's forget it move on' 'I don't think I can' 'everyone makes mistakes'.
They ventured into the bedroom to chat in private.
'You know how I've always felt about you' 'I know'.
'You've got to push away these feelings' 'I can't you know how I've always felt' 'it's wrong' 'I know I can't help it'.
'And I'm trying to ignore how I feel I just need one last kiss' 'Daniel' 'please I can't move on otherwise'.
He leaned in to kiss her passionately Corey didn't feel anything her brother had tried to rape her.
Now she was expected to forget anything had happened.

She could tell he wanted more 'mind if I get a drink?'. Corey asked 'go ahead' Polly said Corey got herself a glass of orange juice as Stacey joined her in the kitchen. 'What's going on I just saw you and Daniel kissing'. 'Corey panicked Stacey had seen them 'it's not what you think he kissed me he came on to me' 'but why?'. 'He just did I don't want to talk about it ok!' Corey decided to leave with Daniel earlier than planned. As she could tell Stacey was confused as she left that night she found it hard to get to sleep worrying about things. As Corey left Stacey wondered about what she'd seen. She sat there with her drink as Polly tidied up 'are you ok?' Polly asked noticing her staring into space. 'Do you know about Daniel and Corey?' 'what do you mean?' 'I saw them kissing' 'what do you mean?'. 'In your bedroom not just a peck on the lips' 'are you sure?' 'positive' 'are you serious?' 'yes' 'no not Cor'. 'Yes' 'but she's gay' 'yeah well look at Steve then I'd say more bi-sexual with a preference for women anyway'. 'There must be an explanation it's incest isn't it illegal?'. Polly said 'I hate that we know this' 'sorry Susie I had to talk to someone' 'I know what shall we do or say?'. 'We could talk to her ask her what's going on'. Polly sggested 'maybe they shared a kiss'.

'I'm not saying it's right but they never had sex we should talk to her' 'ok Susie'.

The next day as planned Polly decided to chat to Corey about things after lunch 'hey Cor' 'hi'.

'I don't know how to talk to you about this last night Stacey saw you kissing Daniel'.

'I told her maybe she got things wrong she said she didn't'

'Oh so you both think I'm having a relationship with my own brother!' 'no course not!' 'yes you do!'.

'What's going on? Daniel hit you the other day you lied to cover it up now you know...just tell me are you?'

'No you want the truth?' 'yes' 'he has feelings for me'.

'My own brother' 'Daniel' 'happy now! you know how screwed up our relationship is' 'Cor we're your friends'.

'I don't fancy my brother I never have he likes me'.

'What can I do no-one understands what it's been like for me' 'tell him it's wrong' 'I have'.

'He always finds an excuse to get closer to me his hand around my waist you think I enjoy this!'.

'You think it's normal!' 'then you have to tell him to leave you alone or I will!' 'please don't tell anyone about this'.

'If anyone found out!' 'I promise it's a shame your single'.

'You need a girlfriend to get him to leave you alone'.

'Maybe you're right' don't get upset' Polly hugged her.

'It's ok at least I have my new film to take my mind off things' 'I know you really wanted that role' 'yeah'.
'I think I can do it well' 'you're a great actress' 'thanks'.
'I'm gonna put on weight for the role I'm a size twelve'.
'And I have to be a fourteen to sixteen it's a film about a slimming club' 'I know you'll be amazing'.
At that moment Daniel walked in 'coming to the studio for a songwriting session' he asked 'yeah ok that's all'
'Stacey' Polly said noticing her on the doorstep 'hi'.
'Well I'm off to the studio for a few hours' 'have fun'.
Stacey said sarcastically 'we will' Daniel said Corey put her head round the door as she looked at Stacey.
She shut the door as they left 'we had a chat' 'so she didn't deny it then' 'he's got feelings for her she was really upset he fancies her and she's done all she can to stop him'.
'But he won't listen she's told me she's never fancied Daniel he likes her but he shouldn't'.
'And she needs our support' 'what about you and Kaleigh? she told me you had a row' Stacey said.
'What else did she say?' 'that you said your mum and her deserve each other'.
*'That you told everyone in the family to f**k off'.*
'It had nothing to do with Kaleigh it was mum I was angry I feel really bad please tell Kaleigh I'm sorry'.

'I tracked down her daughter Harmony I got close to her adoptive mum Vanya I went to her house'.
'Everything was fine mum kept saying how I'd end up hurt if I got too close me and Vanya'.
'Became really good friends she gave me photos of Harmony mum said what would happen'.
'If she knew the truth about Shaun I lied I said it was some lad from school the father'.
'Everything would have been fine so guess what mum does goes and tells Vanya about what happened to Kaleigh'.
'That Harmony is the product of a rape that's it she sends me a text telling me never to see her again'.
'Or go to the house she's the sweetest little girl' 'Susie'.
'Why did you never talk to me? I knew you had that photo'.
'That you gave to Kaleigh' 'I was hoping Kaleigh would see her one day she never will because of me'.
'It's not your fault' 'I saw her in Liverpool in the shopping centre we got chatting she was upset'.
'Harmony asked me why I couldn't come round the house anymore I said I'd always be her friend'.
'That she could see me on TV Vanya's sister was there'.
'She was horrible to me she said if I ever go near the house again she's calling the police'.

'How she's gonna tell her I'm just a celebrity who used to visit' 'it's ok Susie' 'I saw her on Britain's Got Talent'. 'Really' 'yes I was shocked she sang really well I don't know if they'll show it I don't know if Vanya was there'. 'It might have been her uncle' 'you might see her again'. 'I hope so' 'I'll tell Kaleigh everything' 'I'm sorry I ruined everything I should never have contacted her' 'no Susie'.

'You just wanted to know what happened to her'.

'I should have waited till she was eighteen now Kaleigh won't see her'.

'And what if Vanya and her family tell her the truth'.

'And then she never wants to contact us even as an adult' 'I doubt they'll tell her the truth would you?'.

'Why couldn't mum have stayed out of it tell me one good reason why she needed to tell her the truth'.

'Why she did it out of spite only she's hurt Kaleigh'.

'I hate my mum I don't want to see her ever again I'm sure she'll come round here once she knows...' 'knows what?' 'I'm keeping it quiet me and Margie we're having a baby'. 'You're adopting a child?' 'no I'm pregnant' 'this is great news how?' 'a male friend third time lucky'.

'How far gone are you?' 'like five weeks I'm waiting till I'm ten weeks gone before I announce anything'.

'I understand' 'just tell Christian no-one else' 'of course'.

'This is great you can have the best baby shower ever'.
'Let's not get ahead of ourselves anything can happen'.
'I know but it's exciting!' 'we're really happy Margie wants a girl I want a boy we'll see what happens'.
'Well congratulations' 'thanks Stace' 'it's really exciting news' 'are you gonna see Cor' 'ok maybe later'.
'I'll go to the recording studio see if she's there'.
'Oh she was never broken into Daniel smacked her in the face' 'why?' 'he's jealous'.
'Of her close friendship with Steve I don't know the details but she's a bit upset at the moment go easy on her',
Later that afternoon Stacey went to find Corey at the recording studio as she was drinking apple juice.
'Are you free?' 'to record' 'no chat I'm sorry for being off with you Polly said Daniel likes you and he fancies you'.
'Something like that' 'how long?' 'years so my family can't get any worse my dad is in prison'.
'For every crime there is my mam who never loved me'.
'Because I wasn't really her daughter my son who I thought was my brother now my real brother'.
'Wants to screw me' 'why? I never thought Dan was like that he's kissed you before?' 'oh yes'.
'Every innocent peck on the lips every time it reminds me why we don't have a normal relationship'.

'Like other brother and sisters now you know my family secrets the one I never wanted anyone to find out'.

'Polly said he hit you why would he I never knew he was like that has he done it before?' 'dad and Daniel'.

'I should be used to it by now' 'no-one should ever hit a woman' Stacey held her tight 'he's coming'.

'Act normal' 'hi Dan' Stacey said cheerily 'hi Stacey'.

'Recording today?' 'no I haven't chatted to Corey in a while we're having a girlie catch up' 'oh right'.

'We'll take a break' 'great' 'back in twenty minutes'.

Dan left without a care in the world 'you should have told me all this' 'how can I tell people'.

'That my own brother fancies me my councillor and Steve are the only people I've ever told'.

'Well I'm glad you told me tell him you're not comfortable about it with his advances' 'I wish'.

'I've been trying for years it's got to the point where I don't even know if I want to see him'.

'If we can have a normal relationship' 'why did he hit you?' 'we got into a row' 'why?' 'the Las Vegas wedding'.

'He went mad I'd been drinking he realised Steve still fancied me'.

'Dan he couldn't take not being the only man in my life'.

'So he smacked me in the face I tried to cover for him'.
'Margie saw my bruise' 'it's physical assault!' 'I know!'
'Against a woman not just any woman his own sister'.
'You could tell the police' 'then everyone would find out'.
'Maybe they should' 'they can't!' 'what if he hits you again?' 'I'm worried he will or worse'.
'What do you mean?' 'it's nothing' 'tell me please don't go through things alone I'm your best friend'.
'He wanted to have sex with me he forced himself on top of me' 'he raped you!' 'no he threatened to'.
'It's ok he's apologised let's leave it' 'if you can leave it?'.
'Please!' Corey reached for a tissue 'I'll never let anyone hurt you again' Stacey said facing Corey.
As she held her tight they lay on the sofa together as they kissed after a few seconds they stopped.
As Stacey held her close she felt Corey was going through a bad time in her life she offered her love and affection.
She reminded herself she was helping Corey to feel better.
Just a kiss and a cuddle she hoped Corey would find someone nice to be with.
Corey realised she was still in love with Stacey but could never have her.
She realised being with Steve would be the best option.
He would look after her unconditionally.

Corey wanted things to be ok again she decided to fly to L.A she checked into a hotel with her two daughters.
The next day she went to see Steve hoping he'd be in she arrived around 11am.
The girls were fascinated by a water feature in the garden.
Corey ushered them away in case Steve had guests inside they crossed the road 'go to the front door' they ran along.
As Corey ran out a car appeared screeching she hit her head lightly on the front of the car as she lay on the floor.
The car door opened 'Corey are you ok?' 'Kieran'.
'I'm so sorry!' 'I just hit my head I'll be ok' 'I'm so sorry'.
'I never saw you' 'I'll be fine' 'did you hit your head hard?' 'not too bad' 'hey are you ok?' it was Steve.
'I'm ok' Corey stood up 'it was my fault I didn't see Corey'
'I'll be ok I came to surprise you I have the girls with me'.
'I can see that I'm happy that you came'.
'I thought you might be busy or with guests' 'no guests'.
'No women in fact Kieran's my date most nights come in'.
They went inside to Steve's house as they chatted drinking lemonade Steve of course was happy to see Susan.
'Listen I'm sorry about the whole Vegas thing' Corey said.
'Really it's ok' 'no I think we should have planned things properly' 'and it didn't help my brother being there'.
'He's very protective of you' 'he's a fecking psycho!'.

'In fact I'd rather not see him again but he's apologised'.
'I'll give him that anyway what do you say we get married again in Ireland in a church I know a female vicar'.
'Just the two of us and Kieran if he wants to come maybe one of my friends I've done the white wedding thing'.
'So have you what do you think?' 'I'd love to marry you'.
'Even though I upset you in Vegas' 'just a bit but it wasn't your fault you're right we should have planned things'.
'I think it sounds like a nice idea' 'I sold my outfit from my wedding to Polly I have another outfit' 'sounds great'.
'I'll get a suit ready when?' 'whenever you're free'.
'The end of this week' 'let's do it' Steve kissed her.
When he kissed her it felt nice not sleazy like when her brother did as planned a week later they flew to Dublin.
So she could return home and marry Steve they requested to be married at eight
She'd always been a nightbird and often did a lot of recording at night Corey decided to wear an ivory dress.
And lace trainers she loved the outfit she her make-up was nice with blue pastel eye shadow berry coloured lipstick.
Diamond earrings she was so happy Kieran and her old friend Violet were there a nice atmosphere in the church.
As Corey reached the top of the alter she faced Steve.

'Do you Corine Carol Marie O'Hanlon take
Steve John Miller to be your wedded husband' 'I do'.
'You may kiss the bride' as Corey kissed Steve she was on
cloud nine her perfect secret wedding.
She'd done the right thing Steve's mum wouldn't be happy
if she found out as he was Jewish.
The gay community would hate her if they knew she'd
married a man.
Everything had worked out for the best.
'What do you say we get out of these clothes and go
somewhere?' Corey suggested 'like a club' Kieran asked.
'I know a great club' Corey said 'ok let's do it' Steve said.
They changed into more appropriate clothes as they hit the
night clubs choosing one of her favourites.
Corey was so happy nothing could stop her happiness.
As they danced together Corey spied her old friend Colin.
'Corey' 'Colin' 'I haven't seen you in ages' 'I know'.
'We must catch up' 'this is Kieran you remember Steve'.
'How are you?' 'I'm good' 'you on holiday?' 'something
like that I'm showing them the Dublin night scene'.
'Well I bet it doesn't compare to the clubs in America'.
'A party is a party wherever it is' Kieran said 'that's true'.
'You're brother's round here somewhere' 'really where?'.

'Over there' Corey looked over she still couldn't see him 'what have you been up to?' Corey asked.
'I'm engaged now she's a fellow jockey' 'that's good'.
'Your in the same business' Corey said 'thanks'.
'Back in a minute' Corey said looking at Steve she spied her brother at the bar 'I'll be one minute'.
Corey needed to speak to Daniel she couldn't have everyone knowing her business in a club.
And she didn't want another row with him 'Dan'.
'Here alone?' 'with friends' 'what friends?' Daniel looked around 'what are they doing here?'.
'I thought you would have come to your senses by now'.
'Colin's here it's just friends together' 'that's not what you said about Steve' 'I've realised you were right'.
'It might be exciting at first our relationship but it wouldn't last I kissed a girl the other night'.
'It was exciting it's who I am Steve it was just a bit of fun'.
'I made out it was more serious to make you jealous'.
'Well it sounds like the old you is back does Steve know it's not serious?' 'he does now'.
'What's he doing in Ireland?' 'we have a child together'.
'I have no reason to go to the States' 'ok let's move on'.

'I hate this arguing between us you know you're my best friend' 'yeah let's move on'.
Corey was pleased with herself she'd fooled her brother.
He believed she was over Steve inside she could never forgive him for attacking her.
But she didn't want any arguments as long as he didn't come on to her everything would be ok.
That night she had a kiss and a cuddle with Steve.
They were married Polly was now almost seven weeks pregnant.
But she still wouldn't allow herself to get too excited.
In case something happened the row with her mum still playing on her mind.
If only Kaleigh hadn't been caught up in their row.
She'd told Stacey she was sorry but it wasn't the same as seeing her sister she was worried.
What if their mum had told Kaleigh not to speak to her.
If only she had kept out of things now she'd ruined everything she had to talk to Kaleigh.
Polly wasn't happy when Sarah announced she was coming round as Kaleigh had some interviews to do.
For her new single in London and they should talk.
It was the last thing she felt like doing she never wanted to speak to her mum again she made her feelings clear.

Even since she split up with Corey their relationship had gone sour she could have been more understanding.
And she wasn't instead judging her making her feel bad about everything.
Polly couldn't stand her mother's obvious preference of Kaleigh over her for years she'd put up with it.
Now she didn't want to anymore as she waited for her mum to arrive at midday.
Polly hoped she wouldn't stay long ass she heard a knock at the door 'hi look the other day'.
'We both said things we didn't mean' Sarah said acting as if nothing had happened 'speak for yourself' 'come on'.
'I'm your mum let's forget what happened move on'.
'Alright' deep down she didn't want to forget what had been said 'you look good' 'thanks'.
'Is it me or do your boobs look bigger is there something you want to tell me' 'no' 'I know' 'know what?'.
'That you're pregnant you should have said no wonder your hormones were all over the place'.
'How did you find out?' 'your dad told me alright don't be angry I'd like to know why you didn't tell me'.
'I'm only seven weeks gone I don't want everyone finding out' 'they won't I won't tell anyone'.
'I bet you've already told Hilary'.

'Which means she'll have told her mates which means the press will find out' 'I'll make sure they don't I promise'.
'How are you gonna do that?' 'I'll speak to Hilary'.
'You're secrets safe with me my second grandchild'.
'Oh so Susan and Marie don't matter because Corey gave birth to them' 'no darling I love them both'.
'But this baby will be special' 'it's still early days'.
'I know why didn't you tell me?' 'I didn't tell anyone'.
'Not even Stacey in case I couldn't get pregnant'.
'I think it's great' her mum had clearly only come round because she'd found out she was pregnant.
She also hadn't mentioned Harmony as if she didn't exist.
Polly missed her already 'have you talked to Kaleigh?'.
'Not yet' 'you need to apologise for the other night'.
'I've talked to Stacey said I'm sorry' 'it's not good enough she's upset she thinks her sister doesn't love her anymore'.
'Let's forget about what happened focus on this family'.
'She is our family just because Harmony's adopted'.
'Susie please! Vanya wants nothing to do with you Kaleigh's upset let's put this whole thing behind us'.
'No I won't you ruined everything telling Vanya about Shaun! everything was going fine'.
'Before you got involved' 'Kaleigh never asked you to track her down neither did I!'.

'You didn't see how happy Kaleigh was when I gave her the photo Harmony is her daughter'.
'You shouldn't have made her believe she'd meet Harmony' 'she could have'.
'If it wasn't for you ruining everything!' 'she's your niece'.
'Not even that now you've got a baby on the way focus on that' 'please go you're causing me stress'.
'I'm telling you this for your own good you're obsessed with this girl'.
'Who you have no chance of ever seeing again'.
'You're just upsetting yourself' 'you upset me!'.
'I'm looking out for you and I have to look out for Kaleigh I'll go now let you have a think about things'.
'I'll see you tomorrow 'Polly hated her mum she would never forgive her for ruining things with Harmony.
She also didn't care that she was upset over their row all her mum cared about was her own opinions.
If her mum really cared about Kaleigh she would have stayed out of things.
The following day Sarah said she was too busy accompanying Kaleigh on her promotional trip to London.
For her new single to come round Polly was glad.
She wanted to speak to Kaleigh alone without their mum Corey had returned to London.

That evening Polly had suggested they all go out for a meal at a restaurant in London.
Along with Kitty, Daniel, Margie and Carol everyone had dressed up they arrived in good spirits 'table for six'.
The manager said they followed him as they ordered starters of soup and bread which tasted delicious.
Then the main course 'this is nice all of us' Kitty said.
'It's great I can't remember the last time we all had a meal like this' Polly said 'food's great' Corey said.
'Don't you have to put on weight for the film' 'yes'.
'So I'll be eating out more it'll be fun I love my food no more counting calories for a while until the films over'.
'Looks like we'll be...' Polly said as she stopped herself.
'What?' Kitty asked 'I may as well say it since mum knows I'm pregnant' 'congratulations' Kitty said.
'I'm only seven weeks I'm waiting till I'm ten weeks to announce it' 'it's great news let's have a toast'.
'To Polly and Margie' Corey said 'so Cor anyone special in your life?' Kitty asked 'no' she lied 'what about Steve'.
'He came to Ireland just to see you' Daniel said 'we have a child together' 'you know what he wants'.
'Look a few years ago we had a one off relationship'.
'I'm over it I'm looking for a woman' 'we'll find you a woman' Kitty said.

Corey was angry that her brother had mentioned Steve again as they ate dessert 'you won't be as sexy'.
'When you put on weight' Daniel said why couldn't he leave her alone 'it's for a movie'.
'And what's it to you!' 'is he upsetting you?' Carol asked.
'Why is she asking that for? what have you said?'.
'Don't do this!' 'you're the one! telling things to your mam!' 'let's talk outside' Corey got up 'come on!'.
'Unless you want everyone to know our business!' 'fine!'.
He followed her as they talked outside 'what was that about? I think they had some kind of row' Kitty said.
Polly said as almost everyone at the table knew what was going on outside Corey followed her brother.
'You told her things about me!' 'I was upset the night you almost raped me!' 'I never raped you!'.
'I don't know what you would have done unless mam came round she saw me shaking upset'.
'So she took me to her house and Margie saw my bruises when I had a beauty treatment'.
'You think I want people to know our business!'.
'Course not it's how I feel there's nothing wrong with it'.
'It happens all over the world I want to be with you'.
'No-one has to know!' 'you're sick!' 'you kissed me back!'.
'Why are you doing this!' 'don't tell me'.

'You've never wanted me' 'no how long have you fancied me?' 'since I was seventeen I've waited my whole life'.
'To tell you how I feel' 'now you have' 'I'm sorry if it makes you feel uncomfortable' 'yes it does'.
'I'm not yours to have and I never will be and yes Carol and Stacey know how you feel about me' 'Stacey!'.
'Who else knows about this?' 'she saw us kissing that night at Polly's house you're lucky it wasn't anyone else'.
'This fantasy you have about me it stops now!' 'I can't stop how I feel about you and if you tell anyone else'.
'I'll tell people about Steve' 'I already have in my biography I've written about our relationship'.
'What have you said?' 'that I had a relationship with him'.
'After I split with Polly Stacey it's all there my days as an escort girl the band my acting career'.
'Mam Carol Douglas you name it it's there it's a great read coming out in October'.
'If you want me to leave you alone I will' 'I'd like us to have a normal relationship'.
'If not I'd rather you stayed away from me' 'if it's how you feel' 'yes it is let's go rejoin the others'.
'Else they'll be wondering where we are' as Corey rejoined the table she felt better speaking to her brother. She now had the upper hand she'd said her piece.

'Is everything ok?' Carol asked 'great' Corey said 'whatever it is you two need to make it up' Kitty said unaware of the situation 'we will' Daniel assured her after dinner was finished nothing was said. That evening they went to Polly's house hopefully her brother would finally get the message.

They all relaxed in the living room Corey wanted the night to be over so she didn't have to see her brother again. He clearly would never get over his feelings for her.

'Cor' it was Kitty 'what happened at dinner?' 'nothing'.

'You went off to chat in private' 'it's fine' 'it didn't look fine to me' 'we had a row and we've sorted it'.

'What was the row about?' 'I can't say' 'I'm one of your best friends' 'if I could I would' 'why can't you then?'.

'It's a private family matter' 'I'm Dan's wife your sister-in-law so I'm not family now' 'trust me on this'.

'I wish I could tell you' 'the other day you said on Facebook you don't want to play with the band anymore'.

'I said I just need a year off to focus on my solo career'.

'Then you never know' 'you've always said you love being in the group how it's like a marriage'

'How you'd never leave what happened?' 'you know when I'm singing alongside you I'm never happier'.

'Then why would you want to leave?'.

'Things have been a bit strained lately with Dan he's not himself' 'I think it's my fault'.
'I told him I probably can't have kids he wasn't happy'.
'He got angry I've never seen him like that before I could have lied about it not said anything'.
'I thought the truth would be better I shouldn't have said anything' 'he would have found out eventually'.
'When you went to the doctors for tests' 'I know I've never seen him so angry' 'how angry?' 'he got a bit aggressive'.
'I've never seen him like that before he's apologised now'.
'It's ok we can always adopt I'm sure once he gets used to things he'll see we have other options'.
'He still shouldn't have got angry it's not your fault'.
'You can't have kids' 'it's fine now' 'that's good'.
'So you won't leave the band' 'no not if you don't want me too' 'then everything's good'.
How could Corey tell Kitty why she didn't want to play with the group anymore the truth about Daniel.
Polly was enjoying the Britain's Got Talent auditions.
She was enjoying going round the country doing auditions they were spending a few days at each venue.
They had a few more days to go it was hard not being able to tell anyone she was pregnant.
Especially since she had some sickness.

She did have some pills Polly hadn't spoken to Kaleigh. And hoped her mum hadn't turned her against her on a day off she travelled to Manchester.
Where Kaleigh was doing some radio interviews.
As she arrived at one of the radio stations Kaleigh finished the interview taking her headphones off.
Kaleigh saw her at the window as she left the studio.
'Can we chat?' Polly asked 'yeah' 'mum's not here'.
'No' 'good come with me we'll have a milkshake'.
'What do you say?' Polly asked 'yeah ok' they got into a taxi together as they headed into Manchester 'I'm sorry'.
'About that row at Sam's birthday it was mum I was angry not at you I want you to know I love you I'm sorry'.
'It's mum we don't get on' 'it's ok' 'are you sure?' 'yeah'.
'I thought you hated me' 'no you're the best sister in the world I'm just upset I can't see Harmony'.
'I really wanted you to meet her' 'have you still got her photo?' Polly asked 'no' 'why not?' Kaleigh looked upset.
'What's wrong?' 'she threw it away mum' 'how could she!' 'she said...' 'wait a minute'.
'Let's go somewhere more private' 'could you stop here?'. Polly asked the taxi driver 'yes' he stopped as she paid him outside it was raining.
They quickly made their way inside a coffee shop.

'Sit down I'll get us some milkshakes' Kaleigh found a table Polly ordered as she returned.
'I got some coffee cake I thought you might want something to cheer you up' 'thanks'.
'Why did mum throw the photo away?' Polly asked.
'She said we weren't to mention her name that Vanya would never let us anywhere near her'.
'That we had to forget about her' 'Stacey said you looked at that photo everyday' 'yeah she ripped it up'.
'Threw it in the bin mum wants me to forget about her'.
'Do you?' 'now I wish I had the photo it's gone forever'.
'Maybe you don't need a photo maybe we could see her'.
'How?' 'me and Margie saw Vanya's sister in town'.
In Liverpool I chatted to Harmony she saw me she went mad you know'.
'You would have thought I'd killed someone anyway this is all mum what she said she had no reason to tell Vanya'.
'The truth I said it was a lad from school she believed me mum must have been jealous of my friendship with her'.
'Anyway I've just thought of an idea how we can see Harmony' 'how?' 'let's go visit her school'.
'Do you know it?' 'yeah I went with Vanya once'.
'If we went at lunchtime end of school is too risky and Vanya would be there let's go I'd love you to meet her'.

'What's she like?' 'she's sweet shy like you'.
'You'll love her' 'ok' Polly was happy she'd cheered up her sister she couldn't believe how cruel her mum was.
Ripping up Harmony's photo tomorrow could be the day she made Kaleigh's dream come true.
Polly decided to dress conservatively wearing a navy blue coat some black ankle boots.
They both made sure their make-up was perfect in case they were recognised they found the school.
Calling a taxi as they got out 'listen you wait here'.
'If we both get recognised you wait by a tree and when you see me come out' 'alright' Kaleigh said.
Polly walked into the school it seemed nice with wooden flooring art work on the wall.
She spied an empty art classroom a teacher inside.
'Hi' 'hello' 'I'm looking for Harmony Roberts do you know her? curly brown hair' 'oh yeah'.
'Do you know where she might be?' 'she'll be outside'.
'She usually hangs out in the playground after lunch'.
'I'll look there thanks' Polly walked around looking out for anyone that could be her finally she saw her.
In the playground 'Harmony' 'hi' she smiled.
'I hope you don't mind I came to see you I was passing through the area I thought I'd say hi'.

'You were really good on Britain's Got Talent' 'thanks'.
'I think you're gonna do really well on the show I love that song you sang 'Wish Upon A Star' 'I love it too'.
'Listen I've got someone I want you to meet wait here'.
'I'll be one minute' Polly rushed over 'Kaleigh' 'yeah'.
'Come with me I've found her' 'what do I say?' 'you don't have to say anything I'll do all the talking'.
Kaleigh smiled as they walked over 'trust me'.
'It'll be fine we're back this is my sister Kaleigh' 'hi'.
'So what classes do you have today?' Polly asked 'Art'.
'And History' 'what did you learn in History?'.
'About Mary Queen of Scots and Guy Fawkes'.
'I used to love History at school is it a good school?'.
'Yeah the teachers are really nice' 'that's good'.
'We can't stay long don't tell your mum I saw you she'll be angry at me' 'why?' 'we had a falling out'.
'It's been good seeing you again' 'will I see you again?'.
'Maybe I'd like to I'll give you my mobile number'.
Polly got out her notepad as she wrote down her number.
Ripping a page as she folded it up 'keep this somewhere safe where no-one can find it not your pockets'.
'Or your bag you can text or call me anytime you're ever upset about anything or just for a chat ok' 'yeah'.

'I'll let you get on see you soon bye' 'bye' Harmony waved
Polly was buzzing after seeing Harmony again.
Hopefully she wouldn't tell Vanya 'isn't she sweet'.
'Yeah' 'she's got your pretty face she looks nothing like him' 'she's pretty like her mum don't worry'.
'One day she'll know who we are we have to keep in mind her age she's only ten are you glad you met her?' 'yeah'.
'I am' 'don't tell mum I'm not up to another row' 'I won't' 'better than a photo I'm glad you're happy'.
'I knew you'd like Harmony as much as I do'.
'Mum can't tell us what to do she's part of our family'.
'Whether mum likes it or not one day when she's sixteen and she leaves school she'll track us down'.
'When she starts asking questions about who we are'.
'Then we can tell her who we are not now though'.
Polly messaged Corey her good news about seeing Harmony in secret she was happy for her.
Corey had been invited out by Daniel she wasn't sure.
But he insisted he wanted to make it up with her after everything buy her a few drinks she didn't see why not.
Colin would be meeting them and her old friend Julie.
So it wasn't like she'd be alone with her brother all the time they entered the pub one of her favourites in Dublin.
Corey ordered herself a beer and Julie.

She planned to have a few and it was high on calories.
Beer would help her gain weight for the film.
'I haven't had a beer in ages' Julie said Corey sipped hers.
As she ate some crisps with it 'off for a chat back soon'.
Dan said 'we'll be here' Corey said 'your brother is so good looking' Julie said 'sorry that he's taken'.
'Kitty's really nice' there was a karaoke night Corey watched people as Julie went to the ladies.
Daniel returned 'hey sis having a good night' 'yeah listen I need to go to the ladies watch my drink'.
'Of course' Corey went as she chatted to Julie before returning 'thanks' she sipped her beer.
As she enjoyed the music later she danced with Julie.
As she began to feel dizzy and disorientated what was wrong with her?.
Corey knew she'd only had three pints enough to feel merry she felt like she might pass out at any moment.
'I'm not feeling well I need to go outside' she told Julie.
'Shall I come with you?' 'you stay I'll be ok' Corey went outside she didn't feel herself inside Dan found Julie.
'Where's Corey?' 'outside getting some air she feels ill'.
'I'll go see how she is' Dan went to find her 'are you ok?'.
'I feel sick I've only had three drinks' 'I'm taking you home' Dan drove her home 'you'll be ok'.

'I'll get you a glass of water' Corey drank it 'you need to go to bed I'll make you feel better' he took off her fleece. And her T-shirt to help her cool down and because she wanted to be comfortable the next day Corey woke late. Around 2pm she rarely woke that late even if she went to bed late she never got up later than midday.
She must have been tired Corey got washed grabbing a mint and applied some foundation and mascara.
Before going downstairs 'you're here' Daniel said smiling.
'I don't know what happened last night I just remember ordering a beer did I get drunk?' 'you had a few'.
'I don't usually get up this late' 'it's ok I'll get you some toast and orange juice' 'thanks' she felt better.
After eating something Corey decided she wouldn't drink anything for a while when it came to alcohol.
A few days later she began to wonder what had happened they'd gone clubbing had she been date raped?.
Corey suddenly had a flashback it was very vague.
Daniel had been on top of her in the bedroom had her own brother raped her? she had to find out the truth.
She asked Julie what had happened apparently she'd been ill after drinking and Daniel had taken her home alone.
Corey felt upset at the idea whatever his feelings for her surely he would never sexually assault his own sister.

If he was capable of punching her threatening to rape her. Whether he meant it or not why wouldn't he be capable of date rape? she now wished Kitty hadn't married him. Her brother wasn't who she thought he was Kitty said he'd gotten angry with her what else would he do?.
What if he hit her in future after a row Corey wished she could tell someone.
A few weeks later it was time for the Britain's Got Talent auditions to be broadcast Polly couldn't wait.
And she was also curious about things whether they would show Harmony's audition she watched at home.
With Margie that evening Polly watched closely she didn't see anything until the end.
When they saw what was coming up the next week Polly saw Harmony she'd have to wait another week to see it.
A week later it was shown Polly was so proud of her on Twitter and Facebook everyone was talking about her.
As one of the ones to watch on the show a day later people began speculating how Polly knew Harmony.
A rumour started that she was her secret daughter they had the same facial features same accent.
They were from the same part of Liverpool she had curly hair like Harmony did.

Polly had never thought of things like that that someone would see a family resemblance.
She thought the rumours would go away after a few days they didn't Polly didn't know what to do.
She said she wouldn't be commenting on the rumours she also had her management asking her if it was true or not.
What could she say? Kaleigh was still young and her career was going well she may have been twenty four.
But young girls teenagers looked up to her as one of them.
If they found out she'd had a baby at thirteen it might affect her career.
And the fact she'd been sexually abused Polly thought about lying for her.
She could say she was her mum had her at twenty four.
Had an affair while married to Corey it wouldn't affect her too much she was married to a woman.
Her lesbian fans wouldn't care it wasn't like she was twenty one anymore she told Stacey her idea.
She said she wasn't sure but considered the idea her mum went mad saying the rumours would go away.
And it was a stupid idea she decided to leave it for now.
A few days later she received a text off Harmony asking if she'd come to her dance show.
At first Polly thought what if Vanya was there.

And they started rowing then Harmony begged her
why not she thought about going in disguise.
Polly dyed her hair blonde and wore a navy beret she
wanted Kaleigh to come with her she wore a pink wig.
Hopefully no-one would recognise them Polly was sure
someone was watching them but chose to ignore it.
'Funny how you both love dancing so much' Polly said
to Kaleigh 'yeah it is'.
'I wonder if she's as good as you' Polly said speaking
quietly the lights dimmed the show had started.
Harmony was great as were all the girls they enjoyed it.
After a few songs it was the interval Polly panicked
would they get recognised?.
They stood in a quiet part of the building near the
refreshments as Kaleigh sipped orange juice.
'Think you won't get recognised!' a voice called 'just cause
you've dyed your hair blonde' it was Vanya's sister.
Polly recognised her from the shopping centre.
'Harmony asked me to come so I said yes' 'oh really!'.
'I thought I told you to stay away! you better not come
anywhere near the house!' 'she texted me'.
'I suppose you gave out your number to her'.
'Impressed her being a celebrity!' 'it wasn't like that'.

'How was it then?' 'Harmony wanted me there'.
'I'm not here to cause trouble' 'why is your sister here?'.
'I thought Kaleigh might want to come' 'you thought wrong Vanya is her mum' 'I know that' 'I'll say this once'.
'We're her family when you made the decision to give her up get her adopted no-one forced you to'.
'From the time she was a baby we have raised her Vanya as her mum that's her little girl her daughter'.
'You may be her biological family you mean nothing!'.
'Either of you!' 'there's no need for that!' Polly said
'Let me be crystal clear on this so we understand each other if I catch you anywhere near the house'.
'If I see you anywhere near Harmony texting her'.
'Contacting her there will be trouble that's not a threat'.
'It's a promise! if you'll excuse me I'm going to see my niece and I want you out this building'.
'Before Vanya see's you' 'quick let's go' Polly said.
As Kaleigh followed her 'I'm sorry I've ruined everything it was a stupid idea' Polly said angry at herself.
Kaleigh put her arms around her 'love you Kales'.
'I'm sorry I shouldn't have contacted Harmony' 'I'm glad you did I wouldn't have got to see her otherwise'.
'Everything's gone wrong it's all my fault we won't be able to see her until she's left school now'.

'If she wants to find us how can she say when you made the decision to give her up no-one forced you'.
'She says if we go near the house they'll be trouble'.
'I know that's it we don't want them calling the police she's such a bitch Vanya's sister' Polly said.
'It's not like we're trying to take Harmony away just visit sometimes be a friend' Polly said sadly.
'Looks like it's the end I tried everything we can't do anything' 'it's ok Susie' 'at least you saw her'.
'It's more than some people one day she'll meet you'.
'And I know she'll be happy you're her mum and you both love dancing' 'yeah' 'let's go home' Polly said.
Trying to forget the row with Vanya's sister.
Polly returned home upset she vowed one day she'd meet Harmony when she was sixteen tell her everything.
Until then she'd have to forget her even if it broke her heart Kaleigh had taken things well considering.
Maybe her sister was more mature than people gave her credit for the following afternoon Polly relaxed.
Watching a music DVD she was interrupted by a knock at the door Margie went to open 'who is it?' Polly called.
'It's for you' 'hello Polly' it was the police 'what can we do for you? is everything ok?' Margie asked.
'We're here to issue you with a restraining order'.

'I'm sorry we have to do this' 'is this about Harmony?'.
'Yes if you go anywhere near Vanya Roberts'.
'Or her daughter you will be arrested do you understand?' 'yes I understand'.
'I'd appreciate it if you kept this quiet more for my family than me' Polly asked.
'Mrs Roberts has requested this doesn't go to court'.
'There will be no hearing if you abide by the rules'.
'I will' 'just to make it clear there's to be no contact'.
'By either phone or online and you're not to go anywhere near any of them this is an official restraining order'.
'I understand' 'here are the papers have a nice day'.
The police left Polly knew she'd gone too far that she shouldn't have gone to the dance show.
She just wanted to make Harmony happy 'don't say a word I know I've made a mistake' 'it's ok'.
'I should never have got in contact with her I've ruined any chance of Kaleigh ever seeing her'.
'Or having a relationship with her when she's older'.
'I would have done the same thing if I had a daughter'.
'I know even though I can't stand her sister she's right'.
'Their her family they raised her'.
'Looks like I'll have to forget about her' Polly felt sad.

'When she's older she'll find you she'll be proud to have an Aunt like you' Margie assured her.
'They'll make sure she never ever finds out who we are'.
'If they do then their making a big mistake' 'thanks'.
'I'll make sure everything's ok you've got me' 'I know'.
'At least we've got the baby to look forward to' that day Polly found out Harmony had been pulled.
From Britain's Got Talent despite the fact she'd been a favourite as her family said she was too young.
Polly knew the real reason why but had to respect her family's wishes.
She vowed one day she and Kaleigh would see her again.
Corey had decided to focus on her restaurant for a while.
She and sister Nicky had run a vegetarian restaurant in Dublin for a few years with Nicky as chef.
And she helped with the menu, decor & publicity.
It took her mind off things with her brother that lunchtime she was surprised to see Kitty alone without Daniel 'hi'.
'Hi Cor busy?' 'give me five minutes drink?' 'lemonade'.
'Coming right up' Corey returned with her drink.
'If you're busy I can come back' 'no stay one minute'.
Corey took off her apron 'I'm free where's my brother?'.
'We had a row' 'what about?' 'things you know'.

'He's not been angry again?' 'maybe' 'please tell me he's not still upset over you not being able to have kids'.

'Looks like it I talked about adopting a child he went mad that if I can't have a baby then we're not having any kids'.

'It's not your fault' 'I know I'm thirty four I have what three years until my eggs start diminishing'.

'If I have any at all it's a lot of pressure' 'listen to me'.

'He shouldn't be putting any pressure on you you're his wife he should love and support you'.

'Not be pressuring you to have a child' 'I know Cor'.

'He said if he'd have known he wouldn't have married me can you believe it? I thought he loved me'.

'If I was you I wouldn't be choosing my brother as a life partner' 'what do you mean?' 'nothing' 'tell me'.

'He can't treat women well like he should he's nice enough but behind closed doors' 'what do you mean?'.

'Has he ever hit you?' 'no I mean he's been a bit aggressive lately' 'it's only a matter of time'.

'I was never broken into the bruise Daniel hit me' 'what?'.

'Why?' 'he was jealous of my close friendship with Steve'.

'He wants to be the only man in my life I couldn't tell anyone he's my brother' 'I can't believe it!'.

'I'm worried he might hit you he might not but the way he's been lately I wouldn't take any chances' 'he hit you?'.

'Yes I wasn't going to say Margie saw my bruise I tried to hide it under make-up' 'no man should hit a woman'.
'Is that what your row was about? at the restaurant'.
'Why didn't you tell me?' 'he's your husband' 'so it's wrong how could he? he's been a bastard lately'.
'Hitting his own sister this is low when I see him'.
'I'm having a go at him has he apologised?' 'yes and no'.
'I'll tell him if he ever hits you again he'll be in trouble'.
'Don't' 'why not? you said yourself he might do it again'.
'He'll be angry at me if people find out' 'why shouldn't they I've married a man who hits women' 'please!'.
'Let's just move on' 'no Cor I'll speak to him get him to apologise properly' 'he won't there's no point' 'he will'.
'No don't' 'has he hit you before?' 'no' 'then why are you scared of me having a go at him' 'no reason' 'yes there is'.
'Talk to me' 'I can't ok!' 'you're one of my best friends tell me if he's hit you before' 'he hasn't'.
'Then let me have it out with him it's what he deserves!'.
'Please don't!' 'I will let him know what he did was wrong' 'you can't! tust me please leave it'.
'He has hit you before' 'that's why you don't want me talking to him' 'it's not that' 'then what is it?'.
'I can't tell you here listen mam's coming round this afternoon wanna come?' 'ok'.

'I've made a madeira cake last night you'll love it cup of tea?' 'ok listen Cor'.
'You don't have to protect him even if he's you're brother'.
'The last few weeks I've seen his true colours we'll chat later' 'ok bye' Kitty hugged her.
Letting her know she wasn't happy about what he'd done.
After lunch Corey went to see her mum John and her sister Kelly Mike's mother for a get together.
Corey needed something to take her mind off things.
She was worried for Kitty in case her brother did attack her one night.
And wondered if Daniel loved her like he said he did.
Corey greeted her mum as she helped herself to some Vimto 'how are you?' 'I'm ok' 'good'.
'You know who not bothering you' 'I'm trying to avoid him he's got issues' 'I'd say he has I'm worried for you'.
'I can't even stand to be in the same room as him'.
'I think he date raped me' 'you're joking!' 'no'.
'I've got no proof I went out he invited me I was with my friend Julie I asked him to watch my drink'.
'Then I felt ill I'd had a few drinks I don't usually get ill'.
'Dan said he'd take me home then I don't remember anything I have this vague memory of him'.

'On top of me it's not clear like I was dreaming but I was half awake I can't get the idea out of my head'.
'That night what happened that he did that'.
'What do you think?' 'I think you should call the police'.
'I can't' 'why not? yes you can' 'call the police on who?'.
'Mike asked 'no-one just someone' 'if you can't tell your cousin' 'I can't tell anyone' 'Corey I'm worried'.
'What he'll do next' 'I'll make sure he's nowhere near me'.
'To do anything' 'ok you know what I think back soon'.
'What was that all about?' Mike asked 'nothing' 'it didn't sound like nothing if you need any help with anything'.
'Is it your dad? is he out of prison?' 'not as far as I know'.
*'Who is it then? cause I'll beat the s**t out of them anyone who upsets you' 'trust me it wouldn't help'.*
'Your one of my best friends' 'hey Cor' it was Kitty' 'hi'.
'Are you ok after earlier?' 'I'm fine' 'trying to get her to tell me what's up' 'I'm ok'.
'Cor you haven't been yourself lately' 'Dan he hit Corey'.
'Why?' 'he was jealous of Steve our friendship'.
'Any man I talk to please don't tell anyone' 'oh yeah that makes it ok what he did' 'I'm not saying that'.
'I'll have a go at him for you no man hits a woman'.
Mike said 'let's forget about it' 'what you said earlier that you were worried he might hit me in future'.

'Did you mean it?' 'yes I'm looking out for you he might not I wouldn't risk being in a relationship with him'.
'Hello everyone' Carol said 'homemade cookies' 'I'd love some' Kitty said 'I'm going for some fresh air'.
Corey walked to the garden 'what the hell is he playing at hitting a woman!' 'are you taking about Daniel?'.
Carol asked 'yes I've just found out my husband hits his sister my best friend it's a bit of a shock'.
'I thought I married a nice guy Cor says she's worried he'll turn violent I don't know what to think now'.
'Corey wouldn't lie about things' 'I know' 'he tried to rape her' 'when?' 'not that long ago'.
'You didn't see the state she was in that night she was shaking crying I took her home to mine'.
'To make sure she was ok' 'I can't believe this why?'.
'He was jealous of Steve he also smacked her in the face'.
'They had a row one night all I know is he forced himself on her she was scared if she wasn't in the public eye'.
'I'd have called the police it was awful seeing her in that state' 'why would he rape his own sister?'.
'He's been obsessed with her for years I don't know why'.
'Corey kept it a secret for years she thinks it's her fault'.
'That maybe she said or did something to make him fancy her' 'that's terrible'.

'He's also tried to date rape her Corey told me'.

'It's none of my business but I wouldn't stay with someone like that' Carol left as Kitty took in the information.

'What does she mean forced himself on top of her are we talking attempted rape?' Kitty asked shocked.

'Well I've witnessed his mood swings in clubs over the years he's always been a heavy drinker'.

'He told me he'd cut down on alcohol' 'some people are affected by drink' Mike said joining them.

'My husband tried to rape his sister why would he do this?' 'I don't know'.

'I've always suspected he had inappropriate feelings for her' 'Corey' 'yes' 'there was this one night in a club'.

*'He was drunk he said he wanted to f**k his sister'.*

'I thought he was joking then one day in band rehearsals we're talking which celebs we fancy I said Kelly Brook'.

'Then Dan says his sister has the best pair of tits then another time he slow dances with her'.

'He tried to make out their messing around I thought it was strange the way he was acting'.

'Why you'd talk about your sister like that maybe she's been trying to fend off his advances for years'.

*'And we didn't see it' Mike said 'it's f****d up' 'I know'.*

'I need to hear it off Cor what happened' 'go easy on her'.

'Maybe I could chat to her for you' 'what will you say?'.
'Ask her if it's true make sure she's ok Corey is my cousin our bandmate friend and you know I'm here for you too'.
'Thanks' Mike went to find Corey outside she was sat on a wooden bench 'Corine'.
'I haven't been called that in ages' 'are you ok?' 'yes'.
'I'm ok the bruise is almost gone' 'good you know my opinion of Dan isn't very high'.
'I wouldn't want to affect your relationship with him'.
'I couldn't care less because anyone who treats you like he has isn't a friend to me'.
'And he hasn't acted like your brother' 'it was probably the drink the way he feels about you is that the drink too?'.
'What do you mean?' 'you know what I mean I've seen with my own eyes I've heard the way he talks about you'.
'I think it's a disgrace' 'what does he say?' 'things'.
'That he shouldn't be saying about his own sister' 'tell me' 'are you sure?' 'yes I want to hear it'.
*'He's been saying he wants to f**k his own sister'.*
'What great tits you have I've seen the way he is with you'.
'I never said anything I find it odd he fancies his own sister what he did forcing himself on top of you'.
'How do you know?' 'your mam just told Kitty'.

'The best thing if you ask me' 'I don't want to ruin their marriage'.

'You want her to be married to someone like that'.

'You said yourself he might turn violent' 'we don't know for sure just cause he hit me'.

'Corey when I first met Dan he was one of my closest friends then the last three years'.

'He's really been having mood swings getting aggressive with alcohol he's an alcoholic you must know that'.

'I knew he's been drinking more lately' 'I like a drink'.

'I know my limit he carries on day and night he'll have breaks then he goes back to it he's an addict'.

'The company he keeps nowadays alcoholics womanizers' 'I worry for Kitty the way he is these days'.

'Well if she knows what's good for her she'll leave him'.

'You won't tell Dan you know what he did to me? I'm worried what might happen'.

'Corey I'll make sure you're ok nothing will ever happen to you cause you're my cousin one of my best friends'.

'Thanks' Mike hugged her it felt nice Corey wouldn't tell Kitty what to do it was her life.

She wished she could have her old brother back if he was an alcoholic he needed help.

He had to want to quit drinking Corey hoped he would.

Polly had enjoyed being a TV judge and the live shows had now passed she was three months pregnant.
She was having a boy she'd been thinking of names with Margie they'd decided on Louie.
They couldn't wait to tell him they would be naming the baby after him Polly was sure he'd be pleased.
And happy with their idea Polly was keeping herself busy.
Recording music having singing lessons with Andy and the building work in Blackpool the council had approved.
Her idea to open an American style diner and bowling alley near the north pier.
She'd previously had her uncle Sam helping her but she'd not seen him since the family row.
Stacey had come to see how the work was getting on Polly knew it would look great when it was finished.
People would want to eat there if only for the great surroundings just because she was pregnant.
She didn't want to sit around doing nothing and had also started planning her baby shower for August.
It would be near her birthday yes it would be hot.
But she'd have a great time Polly had planned to have an Alice In Wonderland theme
She didn't know if she'd ever have another child.
And she knew Stacey would enjoy helping her plan things.

Corey had started work on her new film Fat Women which she was looking forward to August soon came around.
Polly had brought herself the biggest fan in B & Q.
And had cans of cooling spray Margie was also excited about their baby shower.
Polly made sure her make-up was perfect she'd chosen to wear an oriental style dress.

The last chapter

Which covered her bump she wore a gold locket Margie had brought her she always appreciated her gifts.
Since her mum never really brought her anything.
Instead preferring to shower her sister with presents dresses and jewellery which she found hurtful.
Yes she was a multi millionaire and could have brought anything she wanted but it was the gesture.
That was important Polly reluctantly invited her mum otherwise she'd never hear the end of it.
In any future arguments the words you never invited me going over in her head Hilary and Sam were also coming.
Sam understood their love hate relationship that he also had with Sarah.
Christian, Louie and George were coming hopefully she wouldn't have to talk to her mum much.
Polly opened the door she may have been five months pregnant but she wanted to look her best 'Susie'.
Christian arrived with Kim 'you look great' he said.
'I tried to make the effort I won't be able to stand for long though' 'we'll all sit on the sofa have a nice chat' 'yeah'.
'It'll be nice we've got champagne of course I won't be drinking' 'they sat down with Polly.

'We've brought you're present' 'thanks' the doorbell rang as Polly got up to answer it 'I can go if you want' 'thanks'. Polly was grateful to her brother for being so thoughtful. 'You sit down' 'I feel bad not greeting people' 'don't worry' Louie arrived with Stacey and Kaleigh. 'Polly's having a sit down' 'Christian's offered to greet everyone for me' 'that's nice of him' Stacey said. She hugged Polly 'hi gorgeous love the dress' Louie said. 'Thanks everyone I'm glad you could come' 'we wouldn't have missed it for the world darling' Louie said. 'It's so nice everyone being here' 'exactly it's rare we can all get together work schedules' Louie said. 'It's a shame Maggie can't come she's seeing some buyers for her apartment in New York'. 'She's really moving back here to the UK?' 'yes but I've said if she wants to visit she can stay in my apartment'. 'In New York' Polly explained 'help yourselves to champagne and quiches' 'where's Corey?'. Stacey asked 'is she coming?' 'she's been ill the last few days' 'I hope she's ok' Louie said. 'She's got medication I would have loved her to be here'. 'She's in another country even if it's just over the sea'. 'It's because of her me and Margie got together in the first place' 'I'm sure she wishes she was here'.

'I hope she's ok after...' Stacey stopped herself 'what?'.
Louie asked 'nothing I'm gonna have some champagne'
Stacey poured herself a glass.
Polly was just about to start the opening of the presents
when she heard a knock at the door it was her mum.
With Hilary and Sam 'hi darling you look great'.
Hilary said 'thanks come in' just being in her mum's
presence annoyed her 'Susie you're getting big now'.
'You noticed I'm five months pregnant' 'don't be like that'
'there's some non-alcoholic punch over there' 'great'.
Her mum talked for ten minutes about how great it was
she was having a baby.
How it would take her mind off recent events how she
heard she'd been given a restraining order.
Polly was annoyed but she wanted to move on but she
refused to forget about Harmony.
Her mum was ruining her baby shower Polly loved it
when they all sat down to dinner.
With Alice In Wonderland themed napkins and glasses as
well as cupcakes that said eat & drink me.
Everyone was enjoying themselves 'so how did you get
pregnant I never asked was it the turkey baster job?'.
Her mum asked 'yes if you must know' why did her mum
have to embarrass her at her own baby shower.

'Can I ask who the dad is?' 'a male friend someone we know' 'anyone I know?' 'maybe'.
'You know what I never wanted you to come to my baby shower asking personal questions'.
'I'm not telling you who the father is if you can't be nice you can go!' 'there's no need to be like that!'.
'It's personal for me and Margie to know' 'I don't know why you're being so secretive' 'anyway moving on'.
'I wanted to thank everyone for coming' 'let's have a toast to Polly and Margie' Stacey said.
Everyone raised their glasses Polly was grateful to Stacey for changing the conversation.
After dinner everyone chatted 'I think you owe me an apology' Sarah said angry 'it's our business'.
'Who the father is' 'there's no need to be nasty I won't tell anyone' 'like you never told anyone I was pregnant'.
'I won't say a word' 'I haven't told anyone sorry it's our secret' 'Andy is it?' 'oh yeah Marcee would love that!'.
'Having a baby with his ex-wife' 'who is it then?'.
'I'm not saying' 'Louie' 'give it up please no-one knows'.
'Not even Stacey or anyone' 'your choice I'll find out'.
*Sarah walked off 'like f**k you will' Polly muttered to herself 'everything ok?' Louie asked 'it would be'.*
'If mum wasn't here'.

'She's trying to find out who the dad is we don't want to tell anyone the father wants it kept a secret too'.
'It's your choice darling' 'I can't even be in the same room as her anymore it's so hurtful her behaviour'.
'Choosing one child over another I understand parents have favourites but to be so blatant about it'.
'I know exactly how you feel my brother was always the favourite it didn't matter what I did'.
'I could never compete strange I get on really well with my brother now' 'like me and Kales I love her'.
'It's mum who's the problem' 'did you mean what you said when you didn't want your mum to come' 'yeah'.
'But I would never have heard the end of it if I didn't invite her it was easier to let her come'.
'You're clearly not happy it's your baby shower' 'yeah it's like weddings people get upset if their not invited'.
'I don't know how dad puts up with her she was alright five years ago we used to get on ok not anymore'.
'Don't worry there's no rule that says you must get on with family members' 'thanks'.
'You know I'm always here for you if you need to talk about anything' 'thanks Louie' 'anytime'.
'Oh do you know what Stacey meant when she said she hoped Corey was ok?' 'she had a falling out'.

'With Daniel it's sorted now' 'I must catch up with Corey'.
'I fancy a trip to the film set' 'yeah me as well'.
Polly had a great time chatting to people receiving gifts.
Her dinner seeing old friends she was looking forward
to the future and meeting her baby.
Three months later she had her son in November.
Just in time for Christmas Louie was happy about the
baby being named after him.
Her son's full name was Louie Elton O' Carroll Margie
and Polly were over the moon the baby was gorgeous.
The little hair he had was strawberry blonde.
Even though Margie had wanted a daughter they were
both happy they were overwhelmed with toys and gifts.
Flowers so many they gave some away to children's
hospitals Stacey was the baby's godmother.
Louie it's godfather everything was perfect Christmas
would be even better Maggie was now living in Brighton.
Polly was happy now they'd be able to see each other.
Two weeks before Christmas she came to visit stating
unlike some of her friends babies.
She didn't have to pretend Louie was gorgeous because he
was.
The only thing spoiling her happiness was her mum she'd
decided to stay in London.

Annoying her by offering to help with the baby she and Margie were fine by themselves.
They didn't need anyone interfering there would be enough to do Christmas week.
There was a never ending stream of visitors to see the baby she didn't mind Christian Stacey or Maggie.
But other family members she could do without her mum Hilary and her girlfriend Margie's sister Tina.
Stacey was visiting that evening a welcome relief.
'Hi Louie' Stacey sat down as she admired the baby 'Orangina' 'Polly asked 'love some' she sipped her drink.
'I'm surprised your mum's not here' 'join the club I can't get rid of her' 'I'm sorry'.
'Don't take this the wrong way but one of the reasons I had post-natal depression was because Jean'.
'She never left me alone I had too many visitors'.
'When I should have been resting or spending time with my baby other people holding the baby'.
'When it should have been me I don't want that to happen'.
'For you to go through what I did' 'I know I want to tell them to go away their so happy to see the baby'.
'What does Margie think?' 'the same as me'.
'That we should be left alone' 'then tell them maybe one visitor at the weekend'.

'Problem with mum is she can't keep out of other people's business I don't get on with mum never have not like dad'.
'It's the way things are' 'I know you probably don't want to talk about you know who but I thought about things'.
'Talks I've had with Kaleigh I've tried to work out why you're mum would have told Vanya what she did'.
'I mean you're mum's always been a good friend to me'.
'But sometimes she has a not so nice side she goes too far' 'exactly mum sees things in black and white'.
'Where as I see the whole picture yeah I told a white lie said the dad was some lad from school'.
'Why did she need to know the truth I was thinking about Kaleigh and Harmony' Polly said.
'Funny Kaleigh never got a restraining order' Stacey said.
'I guess I'm a bit outspoken I never meant to cause any trouble' 'I know Susie'.
'I should never have gone to that dance show it was more for Kaleigh she was dancing from when she was a kid'.
'Just like Harmony if I never met her it would be so much easier I should have waited to make contact'.
'You were curious' 'yeah well it was a mistake'.
'I'm sure Vanya's doing a great job I've tried to work out what it was about her I can't she was so special'.
'The sweetest little girl I see Kaleigh's smile in her'.

'Anyway hopefully one day I'll see her again'.
'I'm sure you will then you can tell her everything'.
'What do you think about me sending a Christmas present?' 'what if you get arrested?'.
'Not if I don't say who it's from if I post it from somewhere else will you help me choose a present?'.
'I'd love to Susie let's go to Harrods tomorrow'.
Stacey thought it was a sweet idea.
She just hoped Polly wouldn't get into any trouble breaking her restraining order it was Christmas.
Surely Harmony's family could make an exception and accept a present from Polly she was her Aunt after all.
Margie wasn't sure not wanting Polly to get into any trouble Stacey was sure things would be ok.
Stacey suggested posting it in Brighton if it was stamped in London or Liverpool she would know who it was from.
They went shopping in Harrods Stacey helped her choose a silver heart locket and some eyeshadow.
She knew most ten year olds were just getting into make-up Polly posted the present.
She knew she'd done the right thing she addressed it from Santa's little helper and sent some make-up for Vanya.
Polly didn't know if she hated her maybe she'd just been in shock over the revelation about Harmony's dad.

Maybe her sister had influenced her decision to get a
restraining order she was a nasty piece of work.
It was Christmas hopefully they'd be happy to receive
their mystery gift Polly knew she was taking a risk.
Sending it and she wouldn't be able to do it again in case
she was threatened with a prison sentence.
No-one could stop her thinking about Harmony.
That Christmas was one of the best she'd been popular as
a judge on Britain's Got Talent she had a new baby.
And she'd even started writing songs again.
In her lyric book New Year's Eve was spent in London.
With Margie on New Year's Day Polly checked her e-mails
everything was shut on New Years.
Surfing the net was a good idea she logged on as she saw
an e-mail from Frances Roberts she opened it.
And was surprised by what she read 'hello Polly'.
'My names is Frances I'm Harmony's grandmother'.
'I know what happened with Vanya I was wondering if
you'd like to meet up in secret just the two of us'.
Polly wondered if she was genuine she hoped so she
replied 'I would love to meet you'.
'But I have a restraining order to stay away from Vanya
and Harmony' Frances replied that evening.
'No-one would have to know we could meet in secret'.

'Somewhere quiet out of town I really would like to meet you talk about things' Polly replied back 'ok'.
'Let's organise a place to meet' deep down she had reservations what if Frances hated her.
What if Vanya and her sister were there she'd removed herself from things since the restraining order.
So she could concentrate on her new baby she felt she had nothing to lose she'd take Margie along just in case.
Anything went wrong she told Stacey who thought she was doing the right thing maybe she could get closure.
Find out how they really felt Polly didn't tell Kaleigh.
As she didn't want to get her hopes up about seeing Harmony again which seemed unlikely.
She was curious what Frances would say hopefully she'd like her they arranged to meet at the Wirral as planned.
Polly was with Margie it was 11am Polly wondered if she'd turn up she was wearing a black velvet coat.
It was cold Sam was looking after Louie a woman appeared she was slim with short grey hair a green coat.
She looked in her sixties 'hi' 'hello Polly I'm Frances'.
'It's good to meet you at last' 'thanks you too'.
They sat on a bench 'not got your little baby with you' 'no my uncle Sam's looking after him' 'that's good of him'.
'It's great these days how things are' Frances said.

‘Gay couples can have kids’ ‘Margie’s got two grown up sons from a previous relationship'.
'And I’ve got two daughters with Corey we wanted a baby’ 'well I think it’s nice’ ‘what about you married?’.
‘I had a husband he died’ ‘I’m sorry’ ‘it was fifteen years ago I’m sixty five I have a good social life and family'.
'It’s not like I’m lonely’ ‘that’s good’ ‘I’m sorry about things'.
'I shouldn’t have turned up to Harmony’s dance show she asked me to go I should have said no’ ‘well she’s a child'.
'You were her friend you used to come round to Vanya’s she said’ ‘yeah I used to have a cup of a tea a chat’.
‘As friends it wasn’t just to see Harmony it was Vanya as well it was nice’ 'so you had a falling out?’ ‘yeah’.
‘Because she didn’t like the fact you’d gotten close to Harmony’ ‘I think so'.
'I just wanted to see what she looked like I told her who I was I thought that was it then we struck up a friendship’ ‘I really liked her then I got a text saying Vanya didn’t want me coming round I was upset'.
'But I respected her decision then I saw Harmony in town one day her sister warned me to stay away'.
'I swear I never wanted to cause trouble take her away from her family I just wanted to be a friend'.

'Maybe I was wrong to contact her I was just curious'.
'It's ok Harmony's never had a dad it's always been just the two of them sometimes Vanya's too obsessed'.
'I'd love it if she had a partner it's been five years I know you have to be careful who you let into your life'.
'Of course you love your child more than anything but it's unhealthy not to have your own life'.
'I don't understand why she'd start a friendship to cut you off 'she never told you about Harmony's real dad'.
Polly asked 'just you and Kaleigh' 'he's not a nice man not someone you'd want around 'tell me more'.
'Kaleigh was raped by her step-uncle my Aunt Sue's husband she was thirteen' 'I'm sorry'.
'No-one knew for years she kept it a secret it's ok he's been done by the police he groomed other girls he's a bad man'.
'I had no idea' 'mum told Vanya out of spite she had no reason to I lied said it was a boy from school'.
'I never wanted Harmony or Vanya to find out who her real dad is what he'd done you won't tell her' 'no I won't'.
'I'd hate for Harmony to know she's innocent in all this'.
'A really nice girl at least I know I'm sorry I understand why she cut off contact with you'.
'Why they gave you a restraining order it's not your fault'.
'Thanks' 'poor Kaleigh I remember on X Factor'.

'She seemed so sweet' 'she is she's back in the UK now don't worry we won't come near you bother you'.
'We know you're her family brought her up adopted her'.
'Thankyou Polly I'll make sure when Harmony's older she knows how much her Aunt cared about her'.
'When she's eighteen if she ever wanted to contact us'.
'It's up to her anyway you've got my e-mail' 'yes thanks'.
'I'm glad you told me everything you can rest assured we'll always look after her'.
'And she'll never find out who her dad is it's been informative meeting you' 'glad I could help' 'take care'.
Frances walked away Polly knew why once the word rape had been mentioned that was it she wasn't family anymore.
'I think you should move on it's a hard situation'.
'So much jealousy involved no matter what you say their worried in case you get too close' Margie said.
Trying to make Polly feel better 'if it was me I'd love someone like you in their life when she's eighteen'.
'She'll be happy to see you again' 'I hope so I need to move on now we've got Louie' 'yeah'.
'Let's go see our little boy' Polly felt she'd got closure.
On the whole matter she'd always think of Harmony as part of her family even if she wasn't.

Kitty had separated from Daniel after the way he'd spoken to her and treated Corey.
She'd put up with his drinking long enough she even thought about having a child by herself.
Corey was happy with Steve while she still fancied women she was happy being in a committed relationship.
She still hadn't told anyone except Christian it was nice in a way keeping it a secret.
Corey knew she'd only have to explain herself Steve told her she made him happy that she was his wife.
He'd also told her he was worth 50 million from his film production company that he'd left it to her and Susan.
In his will Corey had no idea he had that much money no wonder his two ex-wives didn't want anyone near him.
Unlike them she wasn't with Steve for the money.
Her brother had tried to make it up with her and insisted he was getting help for his drink problem.
She hoped he was Daniel was upset about Kitty but she felt he only had himself to blame.
Mike, Corey and Kitty decided to have a night out together in Dublin most people felt down after Christmas.
It would be nice as they entered the pub it felt nice and cosy they had a few drinks Corey had to go home early.
Mike took Kitty home to her hotel.

The next afternoon she came round whatever happened Corey had her friends in her life.
That February morning Kitty took Corey to a local pub in London they played pool Corey ordered a WKD.
Kitty an orange juice 'I know it's early in the day'.
'An orange juice come on' 'yeah I'm...I can't I'm pregnant' 'what! how?' 'I'm in shock too'.
'I thought I couldn't get pregnant' 'I can't believe it'.
'When did you find out?' 'about six weeks ago I've not told anyone' 'why? aren't you happy'.
'You've been wanting to get pregnant for years' 'I know'.
'Not like this' 'tell me' 'it was a one night stand I was drunk' 'these things happen look at Susan'.
'She wasn't planned things worked out ok in the end'.
'I really wish I had a father too it's gonna be hard'.
'I'll baby sit for you you're family will be there so the father isn't Dan?' 'that's over with I've moved on'.
'I thought I was gonna be single for a while enjoy life'.
'You've got the baby to look forward to' 'yeah I'm only six weeks gone you never know what can happen'.
'Don't say that' 'it's true I have to be careful' 'is the father someone you just met' 'no at least I know who it is'.
'Who?' 'don't say anything' 'not a word' 'it's Mike'.

'That night at the pub we went back to my hotel room'.
'We drunk some more wine I can't remember much about it
I know I am I've done the test been throwing up'.
'All the usual symptoms' 'have you told him?' 'no we're
such good friends I'll ruin it' 'he has a daughter'.
'I'm sure he'd love another child' 'you think you're not
sure' 'I think he'll be ok about it'.
'As long as he doesn't ask me to marry him I hate that'.
'So a guy you hardly know ok in my case I do asks you to
marry him proposes to a woman he hardly knows'.
'Based on the fact she's carrying his child come on it's not
the sixties now' 'I suppose some people you know'.
'Want to do the right thing' 'I know but I'd like to know
the percentages of these marriages that actually last'.
'Me too I think he'd be happy this is Mike not Dan'
'I will tell him not right now' Corey was happy for Kitty.
So maybe the situation wasn't perfect but she was sure
Mike would be happy as expected he was.
When she told him two weeks later Kitty had told everyone
not to tell Dan who the father was until later on.
As she knew he wouldn't be happy.
A few months later Corey was promoting her new movie.
Fat Women there was already big interest in the media.
Before it's release Corey had started losing some weight.

She was a size 12-14 Corey felt she'd done a
good performance in the movie.
The director said it was being shown at Cannes.
Corey had assumed since it was a British film about a
slimming group that would have a limited audience.
He had insisted on taking the cast to Cannes so they could
all watch the film together Corey was excited.
As she'd been there before with Polly who was also in
Europe promoting her new album.
Steve had come along with Corey as an actor she was sure
no-one would question why they were there together.
As she posed for photos on the red carpet with her fellow
cast members then she went for a press conference.
With reporters finally the screening she hoped the film was
good and everyone enjoyed it.
If a film was bad it could ruin how well it did at the
box office.
No-one wanted to hear their film had received
mixed reviews Polly joined her for the screening.
'It's your big moment all the cast' 'I know'.
As the film began Corey relaxed a bit she realised from the
start it was a good film with a mostly female cast.
As the film went on she realised she was the one getting
all the best scenes along with another cast member.

Her storyline involved her husband beating her calling her names as she tried to escape her abusive marriage. She'd really poured her heart and soul into the role on some scenes she noticed some people were crying. Weight issues clearly affected many people it helped that the film had a great cast and an amazing soundtrack. As the film ended people stood up clapping Corey felt amazing after everyone said how good she was in the film. And how they loved the film 'now you know why I wanted to get it shown at Cannes' the director said. 'You did an amazing job' she said 'and you everyone loves the film' 'I know' Corey felt great she was happy. For the director and the producers and the rest of the cast 'congratulations Cor' Polly said. 'This isn't what I expected I didn't know I'd be in the film so much' 'you were amazing everyone was'. 'I want to see the film again when you premiere in London I'll be there' 'thanks' 'I know Stacey and Kitty will love it'. Later that afternoon Corey enjoyed the sunshine outside she had arranged to meet Cassie at a nearby café. She'd taken a holiday with Kieran and daughter Mia. Cassie greeted her happy to see her she had missed their private pool parties in L.A 'you look great'. Corey said as she admired Cassie's yellow Ray Bans.

'Me you look great I can't wait to see the film'.

'I don't know if it'll be out in the States' 'trust me if you're premiering at Cannes it must be good'.

'If not I'll buy a DVD' 'thanks we got a great reception'.

'That's great I miss you so much' 'I know me too we'll have to get together again soon' Corey suggested.

'I could come to Dublin or I can see you' 'I'm in New York now left L.A' 'well I have a new apartment'.

'For when I visit it wasn't fair to stay at Polly's all the time' 'I understand we'll get together go to Art galleries'.

'Clubbing just like Sex And The City' Cassie joked

'I still like it L.A but you know some places you outgrow'

'I feel the same about L.A plus I love taxi's no taxi's come on' Corey said.

'And Christmas at the Rockefeller Center New York has the best Christmas trees and ice skating'.

'Let's go ice skating at Christmas' 'I'd love that'.

Cassie agreed Steve appeared 'hi' he sat down.

'How's married life?' Cassie asked Corey looked at Steve smiling 'I'm married to a beautiful woman' 'it's nice'.

'Everyone's happy Polly me I still fancy women Steve is the only man I've ever been attracted to been in love with'.

'Been in a relationship with apart from Colin I was only thirteen so it doesn't count he asked me to marry him'.

'I said yes I haven't found love since Polly Steve's good to me kind my companion not just my husband'.
'We go bowling we have fun together' 'you promise you won't tell anyone?' 'not a word'.
'Even Stacey and Polly don't know we got married in Ireland in a small church' 'congratulations' 'thanks'.
Steve returned 'make sure you treat Corey right' 'I told Cassie you're my husband' 'you make a nice couple'.
'Thanks Cassie' Corey felt relieved telling someone a friend about their marriage she felt happy.
And she'd enjoyed seeing Cassie and her film she wanted to see her again soon.
Corey had another event to look forward to her old friend Violet was getting married her mother had finally died.
And she was free to live life openly as a lesbian.
She was marrying her partner Christy and insisted Corey be bridesmaid it was taking place in Worthing.
Violet had told her she could invite whoever she wanted.
She'd invited Kitty, Mike, Louie, Kitty and her sister Nicky.
It would be a nice stress free wedding.
Corey was happy for her that she was finally able to be herself and marry a woman.
Violet was wearing a lilac jacket and pencil skirt she looked great Christy wore a white dress.

Corey waited in the wings as everyone took their places in the reception room.
The music to Braveheart began her bride was half-Scottish as they walked down the aisle.
Corey wore an ivory dress and Violet's son Jason.
They said their vows as everyone clapped Louie thought how nice everyone looked.
After Violet got into a white limousine with her bride.
Everyone went home until the evening reception everyone returned for 5pm at a beautiful five star hotel nearby.
'This is nice' Louie said to Polly 'it's great'.
'Cor looked great don't you think?' Polly said 'stunning'.
'We must find her a girlfriend it's been ages since you know who' 'maybe she's happy being single'.
'Maybe but she's too pretty not to be with anyone this place must have a few lesbians around' 'yeah somewhere'.
They laughed Kitty joined them with Mike 'hey where's ragdoll?' Louie asked his nickname for her 'Cor not sure'.
'She'll be here soon she looked nice' 'that's what I was saying to Polly what a waste being single'.
'I think she's seeing someone but she's being secretive' Kitty said 'maybe it's not serious'.
'That's why she's not said anything' 'I'm sorry it must be hard with you getting a divorce' 'it's fine Louie'.

'If you want my opinion Dan should stay away' Mike said 'we can only hope that ship has sailed'.
'I'm sorry if I said anything to upset you' 'Louie it's fine' '
'We're gonna to have some food back soon' Kitty said.
'Am I missing something?' Louie asked 'Dan had a go at her when he thought she couldn't have children'.
'That he would never have married her if he knew'.
*Polly informed him 'what a b****d' 'I know I never thought Dan was like that'.*
'So he's had this drink problem a while?' 'it makes him angry and aggressive he never used to be like that'.
'Maybe he had a row with Corey maybe she said she wasn't happy with him and that's why their not speaking'.
'It's not that' 'tell me' 'it's for Corey to say and it was a while ago she's trying to move on' 'I'm her best friend'.
'I know trust me it's a hard subject to talk about'.
'Sounds curious' 'all you need to know is he behaved in a way he shouldn't have that wasn't very nice'.
'So she's not talking to him she's civil but their not as close as they were' 'sounds like it's for the best'.
Kitty and Mike returned as they all chatted amongst themselves Corey turned up in a jacket and skirt.
She looked great 'hi Cor' Kitty said 'sorry I'm late'.
'Take a seat we're glad you're here'.

'You look gorgeous' Louie said 'thanks have I missed any gossip?' 'no darling it's a nice reception'.
'Isn't it odd your at your sugar mummy's wedding'
'Maybe I just see her as a really good friend she looked great didn't she?' 'yes darling loved the lilac'.
'We're not escorts anymore' they ate their meal drinking champagne after they danced to a live band.
Louie decided to talk to Mike 'I'm sorry about earlier mentioning Daniel if I upset Kitty' 'no you didn't'.
'I still find it odd Daniel's not here Corey's always talked about him as her best friend'.
'His behaviour ruined everything' 'they had a row?'.
'He tried to force himself on her if you know what I'm saying' 'no not Corey' 'he's always liked her'.
'More than he should he behaved inappropriately he hit her as well threatened her he scared Kitty'.
'He can't be trusted around women I don't know if he's got help for his drink problem but I love these women'.
'I'm shocked' 'we all were I think she's ok Corey seems really happy at the moment' 'thanks I hope she's ok'.
'She's got us' Louie was shocked he'd sexually assaulted his own sister Corey hadn't said anything.
She'd kept it to herself told her bandmates 'hi dance?'.
Corey asked 'why didn't you tell me?' 'about what?'.

'You know what I'm your best friend your brother tried to rape you and you never said anything thought to tell me'.
'It was ages ago' 'I thought our friendship meant something that you could tell me anything'.
'I didn't know what to do I was scared I couldn't tell anyone in case they thought I came on to him'.
'No-one would think that' 'they might he apologised but I don't really see much of him I'm sorry I never told you'.
'And your friendship means a lot to me' 'well it's good to know' Louie held her in his arms 'if I was straight'.
'If we both were we would have made a great couple' Corey didn't know what she'd do without Louie.
Polly sat with Margie as they watched everyone dance having a great time 'let's dance' Margie danced with Polly.
It was magical she'd been lucky enough to fall in love three times in her life things were good.
Polly had closure on the Harmony situation almost she decided to go to Ireland to promote her new album.
On some talk shows and do some radio interviews she decided to go and see Corey they decided to take a ferry.
Polly figured since it was early summer the sea wouldn't be rough she'd never travelled well on ships.
But managed to find a good spot on middle deck 'this is nice us on a ferry going to Ireland' Margie said.

'I remember I was thirteen the first time I was seasick then' 'well I guess a cruise is out of the question'.
'You never know depends on the ship' Polly was glad when they arrived as they checked into their five star hotel.
That evening they had a lovely dinner and watched TV.
The next morning Polly got ready for her radio interviews.
That afternoon she filmed her chat show before going to see Corey they knocked on the door as she answered.
'Come in' they made their way inside 'have we come at an ok time?' she asked 'a perfect time'.
'We've made homemade pizza with the girls it's in the oven I've got a visitor' Polly went into the living room.
'Polly hello' 'Mrs Rayworth' 'long time no see how are you?' 'I'm great this is my other half Margie' 'hello'.
'Mrs Rayworth was my headmistress' 'it's so good to see you and you Polly you look great' 'no'.
'You don't look thirty five' 'thanks Margie gives me facials to keep me looking young she works as a beautician'.
'I heard you're not teaching anymore' 'no retired it's nice'.
'I keep myself busy' 'that's good' 'I think you're a great actress and singer' 'thanks' 'you gave up acting'.
'Yeah I'm a full time singer now I've always had singing lessons I just released my fourth album'.
'It's nice you enjoy what you do' 'yeah I do I'm sorry'.

'For all the trouble I caused at school' 'Polly it was a long time ago' 'I know it's a hard job being a teacher'.
'I thought about you so much over the years' Polly said.
'Me too' 'I'm glad we've finally met again you haven't changed much' 'no I kept the same hairstyle'.
'I straightened my hair once it looked awful' Polly joked.
'I keep it naturally curly my hair' 'you look great'.
'And Corey I swear you never age' 'thanks you should see Stacey she doesn't look a day over twenty one'.
'Pizza everyone' Corey said bringing in some.
With lemonade 'looks good' Polly said it tasted delicious.
They all chatted Polly had a great time with Corey and Mrs Rayworth catching up on old times.
Later that evening Corey asked Polly to fill out a new work permit form for the U.S.
Corey wanted to be able to go between Dublin and New York and didn't want permanent residency.
In the States she asked Polly to help her search for her birth certificate she wanted it photocopied.
Corey went to get a drink as Polly looked through the filing cabinet as she looked through some papers.
She found what she thought was it Polly realised it was a marriage certificate she looked closer.

Corey's name was printed and Steve's she'd married him
Polly was shocked at her discovery.
She assumed their relationship was a fling now it made sense why she had claimed she had been single.
Why she wouldn't say anything speak about her secret girlfriend it made perfect sense she put it back.
Corey clearly wanted their marriage kept secret.
Polly suspected Corey was worried what her gay friends would think she found her birth certificate 'found it'.
Polly said 'great I was getting worried' 'it's all here' that evening they watched Four Weddings And A Funeral.
They hadn't seen it in ages it was Corey's favourite film.
It reminded Polly love was love whether you were gay straight or bi-sexual.
Over the next few months Polly's relationship with her mum didn't get any better but then it never would.
She still saw Douglas from time to time with Corey and still thought of him as her step-son she saw Victoria.
When she could she was now assistant manager at a designer clothes shop in Dublin.
Kitty had a baby son she named Michael after Mike.
Polly still thought of Harmony but had to move on with her life Kaleigh had her life ahead of her.
That Christmas was another good one.

Polly had planned a New Year's Eve party in Dublin for everyone all her family and friends Corey was a DJ.
As everyone arrived Polly greeted them wearing a silver dress the music was playing.
Purple and pink lights were all around it was the best night of her life as the clock struck twelve.
Everyone sang Auld Lang Syne.
As they looked forward to the future.

To be continued...

English Girl Irish Heart

Polly has grown up in Liverpool without her parents one day when she is thirteen she is rescued from a life in care. And sent to live in Ireland for a better life.
After her mysterious uncle Craig pays for her to go to an all-girls private school outside Dublin Angelsfields.
There she meets best friends Stacey and Romina.
Together they navigate their way through school, relationships and life.

Glamour Girl

Polly is seventeen and is training to be a hairdresser when she is spotted on Oxford Street in London.
As a glamour model as she becomes a celebrity
It changes her life forever but life in showbiz is not all she thought it would be.
When manager Adrian tries to control her career music boss Steve offers her the chance to manage her.
And a new start Polly must decide
if she still wants to be a star.

Spotlight

-

Polly has a successful career as a glamour model.
When she gets a role in a hit movie it takes her career to another level and she becomes a Hollywood star.
Unhappy in her marriage she leaves her husband for close friend Corey.
And she must start another chapter in her life with Corey's parents refusing to accept her sexuality.
And secrets from her past about to be revealed.
Can they have the happy ever after they deserve?

Love

Polly and Corey are happily married when Corey is tempted by an affair their marriage is threatened.
Corey is trying to build a relationship with her teenage son her mother's jealousy threatens to ruin everything.
When Corey clashes with her brother's fiancée will it damage their close relationship?.
Stacey is ready for true love but is her new boyfriend's secret past and soon to be mother-in-law
about to come between them?

American Dreams

Polly is living the American dream with a successful acting career and a house in L.A.
When she and wife Corey divorce they must start a new chapter without each other.
Corey feels lost after her divorce when she finds love with a close friend she begins to heal.
But finds hiding a family secret harder than she thought.
Stacey has a successful career in Hollywood after a major film role happily married to Christian.
Her mother-in-law is making things difficult.
She begins to wonder can love conquer all or is real happiness just around the corner?.

<u>*Chasing Rainbows*</u>

After divorcing husband Christian Stacey begins a relationship with best friend Corey.
When Polly Stacey's step-sister Corey's ex-wife and the person closest to her finds out she isn't happy.
Has it ruined their relationship forever?
Kaleigh is in an abusive relationship with girlfriend Casey she sees no way out until Stacey helps her.
And they become good friends when Kaleigh starts to have feelings for her she wonders does Stacey feel the same?.
Polly has fallen out with Stacey.
When she tries to take her own life Polly knows she must repair their broken relationship.
When Polly survives an abusive relationship when new love Margie comes on the scene.
Is she willing to take another chance on love?.

Out now in paperback & PDF

Ingram Content Group UK Ltd.
Milton Keynes UK
UKHW010928260423
420810UK00001B/164